CHRISTOPHER BUSH
THE CASE OF THE CLIMBING RAT

CHRISTOPHER BUSH was born Charlie Christmas Bush in Norfolk in 1885. His father was a farm labourer and his mother a milliner. In the early years of his childhood he lived with his aunt and uncle in London before returning to Norfolk aged seven, later winning a scholarship to Thetford Grammar School.

As an adult, Bush worked as a schoolmaster for 27 years, pausing only to fight in World War One, until retiring aged 46 in 1931 to be a full-time novelist. His first novel featuring the eccentric Ludovic Travers was published in 1926, and was followed by 62 additional Travers mysteries. These are all to be republished by Dean Street Press.

Christopher Bush fought again in World War Two, and was elected a member of the prestigious Detection Club. He died in 1973.

CHRISTOPHER BUSH

THE CASE OF THE CLIMBING RAT

With an introduction
by Curtis Evans

DEAN STREET PRESS

Published by Dean Street Press 2018

Copyright © 1940 Christopher Bush

Introduction copyright © 2018 Curtis Evans

All Rights Reserved

The right of Christopher Bush to be identified as the Author of the Work has been asserted by his estate in accordance with the Copyright, Designs and Patents Act 1988.

First published in 1940 by Cassell & Co., Ltd.

Cover by DSP

ISBN 978 1 912574 09 4

www.deanstreetpress.co.uk

INTRODUCTION

Before the Blitzkrieg: Christopher Bush's Little Murder Tour in France, 1939-1940

In June 1939 and January 1940 respectively, Christopher Bush published *The Case of the Flying Donkey* and *The Case of the Climbing Rat*, both of them detective novels set in France before the outbreak of the Second World War. Bush, who was fluent in the French language and had visited France many times, held the country and its people in great affection; and it is hard not to see these two crime novels—both of which reunite Bush's series amateur sleuth, Ludovic "Ludo" Travers, with Inspector Laurin Gallois of the Sûreté Générale (the two men had worked well together before in *The Case of the Three Strange Faces*, published in 1933)--as a heartfelt tribute to a nation that soon was to be mercilessly scourged by German invasion and occupation. A little over two months after the publication of *The Case of the Flying Donkey*, Germany would infamously invade Poland, precipitating much of Europe into a state of war. Less than four months after the publication of *The Case of the Climbing Rat*, France herself would be overrun by a seemingly unstoppable Nazi war machine, leading to the fall of Paris on June 14 and the surrender of the country less than two weeks later. Some 600,000 French people would be killed in the Second World War, nearly two-thirds of them civilians.

For his part Christopher Bush, a veteran of the First World War, at the dire advent of the second one went back into military service on behalf of his nation. While France was collapsing under the unbearable weight of the German blitzkrieg and the British Expeditionary Force was desperately attempting to extricate itself from seemingly certain doom at Dunkirk, Bush was administering a prisoner-of-war and enemy alien internment camp across the Channel in a Southampton suburb, an experience the author would partially incorporate into his next Ludo Travers detective novel, *The Case of the Murdered*

Major, which was published in 1941. Neither Christopher Bush nor his series sleuth would see France again for the duration of the war. Doubtlessly for Francophile detective fiction fans like Bush, the charming Gallic glimpses of a peacetime world provided in *The Case of the Flying Donkey* and *The Case of the Climbing Rat* brought back better and far less jaded days, when death could still be treated as a game.

The Case of the Climbing Rat (1940)

CHRISTOPHER BUSH'S series sleuth Ludovic "Ludo" Travers returns for a final pre-war detection engagement in France in *The Case of the Climbing Rat*, a strange affair involving--in addition to a rambling Gallic rodent--a notorious physician relation of his wife Bernice, a celebrated troupe of trapeze artists and, last but most definitely not least, an infamous serial killer by the name of Armand Bariche, compared with whose criminal career that of the notorious Henri Desire Landru (aka Bluebeard) "had been far less horrifying." This is quite a statement, as Landru had been tried and convicted in France in 1921 for the murder of eleven people, ten of them women whom he had cruelly seduced and slain around the time of the Frist World War, after first having gained access to their material assets. Landru is believed to have removed the physical evidence of his terrible crimes by dismembering his victim's bodies and burning the pieces to ashes in his kitchen stove. Naturally the ghastly and grisly Landru case attracted the attention of writers and filmmakers, including Bush's Detection Club colleagues E.R. Punshon (who wrote an analysis of the case in the true crime Detection Club anthology *The Anatomy of Murder*, 1936) and John Dickson Carr (who depicted a Bluebeard-like killer in his Carter Dickson detective novel *My Late Wives*, 1946), horror writer H.P. Lovecraft, who included Landru among the eerie wax effigies in his short story "The Horror in the Museum" (1932, a revision of the work of Hazel Heald) and cinema directors Charlie Chaplin (*Monsieur Verdoux*, 1947) and Claude Chabrol (*Landru*, 1962). The real life Landru was guillotined in France in 1922 and today what is purportedly the slayer's severed head is displayed, in rather dubious taste, at the Museum of Death in Hollywood, California.

The grim spirit of Landru quickly rises, like a spectre from the grave, in *The Case of the Climbing Rat*. In France an anonymous informant contends to the startled Inspector Laurin Gallois of the Sureté that the serial killer Armand Bariche is not dead as is widely believed, but rather roaming free and unfettered, doubtlessly planning something wicked whichever way he comes. Meanwhile in England Ludo Travers is disturbed to learn from his wife Bernice that her shady relation Gustave Rionne is importuning her for financial assistance in correspondence from France, his native country. It seems that Rionne was a Harley Street doctor married to Bernice's Aunt Emily and "one of the very first plastic surgeons who really did anything worthwhile." However, "there was a scandal," explains Bernice vaguely ("something perfectly dreadful it must have been"), and Rionne was struck off the medical register and effectively exiled abroad. To deal with Bernice's regrettable relative (this will not be the last of Bernice's problematic kinsfolk with whom Ludo will reluctantly parley), Travers travels to Carliens in the south of France. There he soon finds himself embroiled yet again in another murder mystery, when a man is found mortally stabbed in the back at a public lavatory outside the circus where the Troupe Helmont--the famous incognito trapeze artists Jules, Berthe and Jeanne Helmont (not to mention Auguste, their climbing white rat)--have been performing. The dead man, it seems, is no other than Gustave Rionne!

Travers learns from his friend Inspector Gallois that Rionne had continued his highly chequered career after departing England, having been convicted and imprisoned for performing an abortion in 1920, served as the defendant in an action brought by a patient in 1933 for causing injuries by his carelessness in a skin-grafting operation and more latterly been expelled from Switzerland for suspicion of drug trafficking. Preoccupied as he is with the Bariche affair, Gallois dismisses Rionne's sordid life and dismal death as a matter of no importance, but the veteran mystery reader may well suspect that there is some link between the doctor's unnatural demise and both the mysterious Troupe Helmont and the murderer Bariche, who seemingly has come back from the dead. Then there is the matter of the suspicious accident which befalls Charles Ribaud, the winning young protégé of Inspector Gallois who was to meet with the Bariche informant—for Ribaud's "accident" appears to have been, rather, attempted murder. When another murder—the shooting of Swiss national Georges Letoque at the Villa Sablons—takes place at a locale "hitherto so free from serious crime as Carliens," the death of Rionne and the attempt upon Ribaud take on a new and sinister significance. What ties it all together? Bariche!

Unbeknownst to each other, Travers and Gallois by different routes simultaneously reach the solution to a rather tragic mystery, prompting the inspector feelingly to tell his friend Ludo: "We are affinities, you and I, and what one thinks the other thinks also." Like Ludo Travers, Christopher Bush clearly had an affinity for France and its people, a feeling which found moving expression in the year 1940 in *The Case of the Climbing Rat*.

Curtis Evans

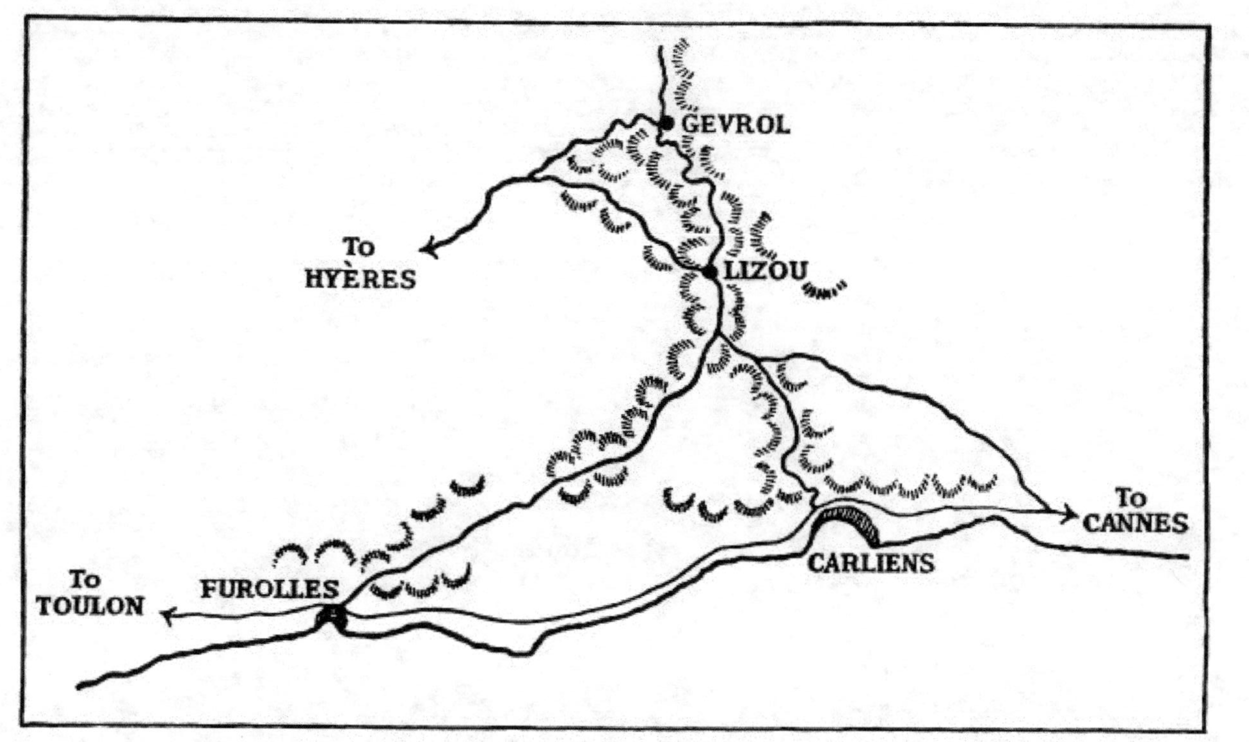

GEVROL
LIZOU
To HYÈRES
CARLIENS
To CANNES
FUROLLES
To TOULON

CHAPTER I
GALLOIS ANTICIPATES

LAURIN GALLOIS was not working that evening, even if he was in his room at the Sûreté. Charles Rabaud, the young secretary and right-hand man, was working busily enough, but the Inspector was leaning back in his chair at the handsome desk, a pencil in his long, sensitive fingers, and a smile, more than ever gently melancholy, on his sensitive lips.

To his intimates, and to Ludovic Travers in particular, Gallois was always claiming that in him were found two wholly different men. Travers was ready enough to agree; indeed, he would have gone further and admitted that he was three. There was Gallois the man of action, brilliant in deduction, tenacious of purpose, and quivering with the sensibility that a case worth his while would invoke. But there was also the Gallois who was bored by the drab routine of ordinary work, whose keen brain felt stifled and hampered by the merely everyday, and who found official forms and documents nothing but a series of emetics.

So much for Gallois of the Sûreté: but there was another Gallois—the artist and poet. Travers always thought that the perfect portrait of him would have been as a virtuoso, painted by John as a pair to that great portrait of Suggia. A violin should be tucked beneath his chin, the bow superbly drawn, the long, lean fingers caught in some dexterity of double-stopping, and on his face that sad brooding smile that had in it a sympathy for all the sorrows of a world.

That evening it was Gallois the poet who was ruminatively at work. There was an intellectual circle to which he belonged, and his turn would be coming in a month or two to contribute a paper. And as Gallois was so much of an Anglophile as to be almost an Anglomaniac, he had gone at once for a theme to some point of literary contact, and at that very moment was deciding on Molière and his debt to Shakespeare. Then the buzzer went. Gallois frowned as he picked up the receiver.

"An anonymous caller on the line, Monsieur l'Inspecteur, who says he has information about Bariche."

"Bariche!" The eyes of Gallois goggled. "Put him through."

Charles, from the side-table, had also pricked his ears at that mention of France's latest and most spectacular Bluebeard, and so that the sound of the keys should not disturb his own listening, was temporarily abandoning his typing.

"The headphones—quick!" Gallois hissed agitatedly across at him. "Paper and pencil. And record in your mind, if you please, your own impressions."

Charles was just in time for the first sound of the voice, and an unusual voice it was—high pitched, querulous and slightly asthmatic.

"You are Inspector Gallois who was in charge of the Bariche affair?"

"Yes. Who is it speaking?"

"That I am unable at present to tell you, but I am genuine—I assure you of that."

"Continue, I beg of you," said Gallois suavely. "What is this information you wish to give me?"

There was a slight clearing of the throat before the voice went on.

"First of all, is there a reward for the capture of this Bariche?"

"But Bariche is dead!"

"M'sieu, I am assuring you that he is *not* dead."

Gallois grunted as if enormously surprised.

"There will be a reward then for his arrest?" the voice was going on.

"Undoubtedly."

"It will be a considerable sum?"

Gallois smiled sadly.

"That depends not only on the amount but on the need of monsieur, if he will allow me to say so. There are those to whom a thousand francs would be a considerable sum."

The listener discerned the subtle question behind the remark and he took a moment or two's thought.

"I would not embroil myself with the affair for a thousand francs. What is the final sum which the authorities would be prepared to pay?"

The shoulders of Gallois drooped and a world of regret was in his voice.

"That, monsieur, I do not know, but if you ring again in the morning I guarantee to inform you."

"There is no hurry," the voice said. "There are certain inquiries which it will be necessary for me to complete."

"Precisely," said Gallois, with the same suavity. "You therefore know the whereabouts of Bariche?"

"I think so, but I am not sure. As I said, there are inquiries which I still have to make."

"The inquiries will take—how long?"

"That I cannot say. A week perhaps. Also it is possible—" He broke off as if to think once more. "It is very difficult to explain, but I ask you to believe me a man of honour. I wish the revelations to be made by a third party, because there are certain confidences which I am bound not to reveal. I am obtaining the assistance of this third party."

"Precisely," said Gallois again. "May I also assure you that I desire to respect these confidences. If monsieur cares at this moment, for instance, to give me merely his name, I give my sacred word that it shall not be known outside this room."

"That is impossible," the voice said with a curt finality.

"Perhaps I could arrange a personal and private interview at any place monsieur would care to suggest. There could also be every possible safe-guard."

"That unfortunately is impossible," the voice said, and with a definite regret. "You are in Paris and I am—a thousand kilometres away."

Gallois smiled sadly.

"M'sieu, if you are twenty thousand kilometres away, it wouldn't matter. Where Bariche is concerned, I should consider it no more than a step across the road." He smiled even more sadly. "But if you wish me to come to Indo-China or Siberia, might you not at least describe this supposed Bariche to me as a proof that your information is genuine?"

A pause. "That, monsieur, I am afraid I prefer not to do. As I told you, there are certain things to verify. Nevertheless I swear my offer is genuine."

"As you wish," Gallois said. "And where and when do you want me to meet you?"

There was a longer pause, then: "You would be prepared to come to Toulon?"

"But certainly."

"I see. If you will allow me a moment then, to make arrangements in my mind, and write them down?"

One minute and he was ready.

"You could be in Toulon this day week? At eighteen hours, at the door of the Bureau of the Syndicat d'Initiative?"

"I shall be there," Gallois told him. "On Wednesday next at eighteen hours. And I shall recognize you—how?"

"I have a photograph of yourself, and it will be I who approaches you. You can absolutely rely on me. Au revoir, monsieur."

"One moment," said Gallois quickly. "This matter of the reward?"

"We can discuss that then. But I should not be interested in a sum of less than fifty thousand francs. If my information is complete, I may desire much more."

"As you will," said Gallois calmly. "That, as you say, is a something which also can be discussed later. Until Wednesday then."

"Until Wednesday," repeated the voice, and at once the line was dead.

Gallois frowned for a moment, then was pressing the buzzer.

"You have traced that call?"

"Yes, It was from Toulon."

"Then take these instructions. Request Toulon to discover the place of origin of the call, and request also that the greatest circumspection should be employed. I'd like the information before my departure to-morrow afternoon."

He sat frowning for a minute before he turned to Charles.

"You think he is genuine, this informer?"

Charles smiled, and one saw at once an extraordinary likeness to Gallois himself, though the snub nose gave the face a difference as well as a curious attractiveness. The scandalous would hint that Charles was more than the great man's protégé and that his adoption by Gallois had had in it more than benevolence, but few could deny the young *agent's* merits or maintain a jealousy in the face of his personal charm.

"Is it not the rule," Charles said, "that an anonymous communication should never be disregarded? Besides, you yourself never believed that it was Bariche who died in that fire."

"And you?" countered Gallois.

Charles shrugged his shoulders.

"Your own conclusions were overwhelming. If our superiors thought differently . . ."

He shrugged his shoulders again. Gallois was walking slowly round the room, his lean fingers feeling, as it were, the air, as if to pluck from it the confirmation he needed. Then at last he halted, and faced Charles again.

"The difficulty was that nobody was ever very closely acquainted with Bariche—"

"Except his victims."

"Precisely," said Gallois imperturbably. "And the dead unhappily leave little evidence. But in that fire a man and a woman died, and the man wore the clothes which Bariche had been seen wearing, and Bariche's ring was on his finger. Both had been shot and it was impossible to say who had died first. If the man was not Bariche, then who was he?"

"But, if you will pardon the liberty, why repeat the conclusions of those who disagreed with us?" Charles asked dryly.

"Because after all they may be right," Gallois told him.

"But there was always the fire. I admit again that there were those who disagreed with you, but—you will pardon the impertinence?—I myself believed your theories implicitly. 'Bariche,' I said to myself, 'pretends to be dead and gets rid of another victim at the same time. Sooner or later he will reappear, and the trouble is that till perhaps many more women are dead we shall not be aware that we were right.'"

Gallois was nodding to himself as he resumed his walk around the room. It was the fire at the Auteuil villa of which they had been talking, with its revelations, through the supposed discovery of the man's identity, of the trail of victims that Bariche had left through France. The career of Landru had been far less horrifying than that of Bariche, and even then the police were of the opinion that many of his victims were still unknown. And another tragedy of the Auteuil fire had been that Bariche—dead or alive—had left behind him never a fingerprint. His methods, too, had been far more subtle than those of Landru. The women he had married were never young and callow, but of an age and kind to manage their own affairs, and he had always succeeded in avoiding personal contact with relatives. Later there would be a letter from the wife announcing a sudden business trip abroad, after which—nothing. And since the various disappearances were not focused about the one man, Bariche, till after the Auteuil fire, it had been extremely difficult for the police to hark back and compile a description of Bariche from the recollections of tradesmen and such others as had seen him or come into some brief impersonal contacts.

Gallois halted again, nodded to himself, and then came back to his seat at the desk.

"Let us leave all that," he said. "This conversation which you have written down—what were your impressions?"

"You assume that Bariche is alive?"

Gallois made a gesture of impatience.

"But certainly."

Charles nodded in satisfied acceptance.

"Then I would say that Toulon is an admirable place for him to make a reappearance. The Riviera is one of the districts from which we had no information about him at all. Also he was not of the crude type who inveigled servants and typists. His women had money and were superior—the kind he would find at this moment, for instance, on the Riviera, during the spring."

The face of Gallois lighted for a moment.

"Admirable," he said. "As you say, this Bariche is the plausible, handsome type, and he has made money."

"It is also well over six months since the fire," Charles said, "and he knows the public has accepted for a fact that he is dead. He would have waited that long to make sure."

"Yes," said Gallois reflectively. "But the informer. What is his relationship with Bariche?"

"There was a mention of secrecy," Charles reminded him, if somewhat tentatively. "He said he had scruples and he wished the vital information to come through a third party."

"Yes?"

"Well, there is the possibility, for instance, that this informer may be a priest."

Gallois looked as if the idea had not occurred to him.

"A priest," he said, and frowned. "Then he obtained the information at the confessional, through some new victim whom Bariche has in mind. But how could that woman possibly suspect that her lover or fiancé was Bariche? The papers announced that Bariche was dead, and only you and I thought otherwise."

Charles shrugged his shoulders again.

"A description was circulated, when we were hunting for information. Every paper published it."

"But a description is not a photograph. Besides this Bariche was a chameleon. The only thing of which we are certain is his height and build, and possibly the colour of his eyes."

"All the same, it is something," Charles insisted. "But if you will pardon me, what good is it to speculate?" He smiled. "I remember an argument with M. Travers, who is what you called the *grand théoriste*—"

Gallois had smiled at the first mention of Travers's name, and at once he was seeing him in his mind's eye. Travers, like himself tall and lean, and in other innumerable ways an affinity. Yet of a type that was essentially English: reticent and with easy optimisms; the perfect listener and the most loyal of colleagues; gravely courteous but with a mind so agile that to propound a problem was indeed to hear some theory of his arrive like an echo.

"In our profession there are all types," he said reprovingly. "When one indulges in theories like our good friend M. Travers, naturally one makes mistakes. But it is the genius of M. Travers that he himself sifts and discards the theories that are wrong, and sooner or later he arrives at the only one that is right. There was a certain *mot* of his—"

"'It is only the fools who are never wrong.'" quoted Charles.

"Precisely. And you yourself, my dear Charles, while remembering the argument, have forgotten the fact that on that same occasion it was M. Travers who again was right and whom I recommended to you as a model."

He smiled dryly as the face of Charles fell.

"You would now tell me perhaps that this Bariche talks in his sleep, or that the woman is suspicious because he is already making preparations to secure her money." He shrugged his shoulders. "But there are a hundred theories, as you say. Let us return then to the informer. If he is a priest, why should he be so anxious about the amount of the reward?"

"You still desire me to theorize?" Charles asked, not without a certain pique.

"But why not?"

"Then if he is a priest, he will consider he is not breaking the seal of the confessional provided he can induce the third party to give information. As for the money, did you ever know a priest who had no use for money? Not for himself, necessarily. For some charity, perhaps, or a religious foundation."

Gallois nodded.

"And his voice? It was that of a priest?"

Charles gave a sly look. Gallois smiled sadly.

"You think you discern a trap. You say to yourself that if he disguises his voice then he will speak unlike a priest. But was the voice disguised?"

"In my opinion—not. And I still think it may have been the conversational voice of a priest."

The only comment of Gallois was to press the buzzer and lift the receiver.

"It is you, Lucien? Then take this down as urgent, and particularly confidential. Ask Toulon to discover for us, if possible, the name of any father concerned with confessionals who has a voice that is high pitched and inclined to break. A tendency to being asthmatical, if they prefer. If there is time they should inquire in the neighbourhood as well as in the town itself. The information to be sent to me personally, at Nîmes, before Sunday next. Repeat, if you please."

He nodded as if satisfied as he hung up the receiver.

"If this priest exists and there is any information," he said to Charles, "it is you I shall send from Nîmes to obtain further information in advance. As apparently he knows me, I must not be seen in Toulon myself before the interview, or he may be alarmed. But one question that occurs to me. You are acquainted with Toulon even better than myself. Why the choice of the Syndicat d'Initiative for the rendezvous? Isn't it near the Place de la Liberté where every one promenades at six o'clock? It is among crowds that one can always be unobserved."

"But the Syndicat building faces the Place," Charles said. "Also it is not central. It is on one side, and you can have every one beneath your eye without being observed yourself." His face lighted. "There is a lounge with a large expanse of glass that faces the Place and I seem to remember maps hung on it and notices of information. Any one could pretend to be looking at those and at the same time be really looking out at the promenaders in the Place de la Liberté. What I imply is that the priest could be out of sight himself and nevertheless be watching for you to approach."

"Excellent," Gallois said. "Make arrangements, please, for us to have a meal here in this room, then bring all the papers relating to the *affaire Bariche*."

The papers came, but before he re-examined them he read again and again that description which had been carefully put together of Bariche as he had been known at Auteuil.

ARMAND BARICHE *alias* Bernard Aiglon, *alias* Hippolyte Defrère, *alias* Guillaume Tréfort, etc., etc, Height 1.57 metres approx., clean-shaven but may now be wearing a moustache and/or beard; colour of hair flaxen, but may have been dyed. Eyes blue-grey. Well built and carriage upright. Voice baritone and slight tendency to lisp. Lips full. Complexion pale. Chin pointed, and with dimple.

As Gallois laid that description aside, he was clicking his tongue with a justifiable exasperation. There on the table before him was the only Bariche he had ever known—a Bariche of shreds and patches and mere words. And then suddenly he was nodding to himself with something of a grim resolve. If the informer were right—and in his heart and soul he believed that he *was* right—then in another week there should be another Bariche, and already his long fingers were crooking themselves and lifting as if to close tenaciously upon the shoulder of a real and living man.

The following evening Gallois left for Nîmes where he was due at a conference. Charles accompanied him—though, when the conference was over, he was hoping to take a short holiday.

It was on the Thursday—eight days before Good Friday, which fell late that year—that the two reached Nîmes. There Gallois learned that the person who had made the long-distance call from Toulon to the Sûreté could not be traced.

The conference itself ended on the Saturday night, but there were various points to clear up and one rather boring function still to attend. Gallois dexterously pleaded urgency of work, and delegated the boredoms to Charles. As a set-off, Charles was definitely given his holiday. On the Wednesday, however, he was to be in Toulon at six o'clock, and on one of the seats of the Place de la Liberté nearest to the Syndicat building. What he did with himself in the meantime was his own affair.

Gallois decided to have something of a holiday while awaiting the Wednesday's meeting. Toulon had been wholly unsuccessful in its search for the supposed priest, and he took the *au-*

tobus to Marseilles, and from there another that went to Toulon and along the coast. At Toulon, during a ten-minute halt, he squinted through the window at the place of the Wednesday's meeting, and was gratified to see that Charles's theory had had a considerable basis of fact.

Early on the Monday the *autobus* that was taking him along the coast arrived at Carliens. Gallois had never been there before, and he found the place irresistibly attractive. Little over an hour in a fast car would bring him back to Toulon, as he told himself, and he made up his mind that he would go no farther. Till the Wednesday afternoon he would bask in the Carliens sun, and at the same time get together some ideas about Shakespeare and the French dramatists of the seventeenth century. From the Hôtel de France, where he booked a room, he once more rang the police at Toulon in case something should have happened since his departure from Nîmes. But nothing had happened. The Toulon authorities had made inquiries throughout the district and there was never a priest with a voice like that which Gallois had described.

CHAPTER II
THE CLIMBING RAT

THERE MAY BE a skeleton in every cupboard, but one would have thought that the Travers's cupboard would have been the last in which to look. With them everything was going well: a delightful home, comfort without ostentation, a wide circle of friends and no possible fear of financial worries. Bernice and her sister were about to leave on a Mediterranean cruise that would last till well over Easter. Travers was to join them later at Marseilles on the return and the three were to travel by road through Paris and so home.

Then almost on the eve of the cruise Travers discovered the skeleton. In some curious way he knew that Bernice was worried about something, but he made no comment and left the moment of revelation to her. He did imagine that the worry was due to a certain letter she had received, and it was when the second letter arrived some days later that she approached him.

"Darling, I'm frightfully worried."

"About what?"

She hesitated. "You're going to be very angry with me."

"Am I?" said Travers. "That will be an event."

"Oh but you will. You see—well, I've kept something from you."

Travers was still smiling. "Really? And what's his name?"

She stared. "How on earth did you know?"

The wind was taken clean out of Travers's complacent sails. He fumbled at his glasses, which was a trick of his when suddenly surprised or on the edge of some discovery. Then Bernice understood.

"It's not a he of that kind. It's Uncle Gustave."

Travers smiled feebly and let out a breath. "And who on earth is Uncle Gustave?"

"Well, you knew Aunt Emily?"

"Your Aunt Emily who died two years ago? Well, I've heard you mention her, but I don't think I ever actually met her." He thought of something.

"She was a widow, wasn't she?"

"No," said Bernice, still somewhat hesitatingly. "She was supposed to be a widow and her name wasn't really Haire. The name was Rionne. She had been married to a doctor called Gustave Rionne."

Travels raised his eyebrows. "French, was he? Or naturalized?"

Bernice frowned for a moment or two in thought. "It's really very difficult for me to tell you all about it. It must have happened when I was quite a girl. He was French. I don't think he was naturalized. In fact I am sure he wasn't. I should have told you Aunt Emily confided all this to me two years ago, just before she died."

Travers was giving his glasses a polish. "Well, what's all the worry?"

"You mustn't hurry me," she said. "You're getting me all muddled up. What was I saying? Oh, yes, that he wasn't naturalized. He was frightfully clever, even Aunt Emily admitted that, and he was Harley Street, if that is anything to go by." She frowned. "I don't think I've got it wrong, but I believe Aunt Emily said he was one of the very first plastic surgeons who really did anything worth while, and then there was a scandal; something perfectly dreadful it must have been, and he was struck off the list, or whatever you call it. He went to France, or escaped to France, and Aunt Emily divorced him, and took her maiden name. About a year before she died she had a letter from him, From Switzerland I think it was, saying he was ill and very hard up, and begging for help, so she allowed him a small pension— about a hundred and fifty a year, I think—"

"Pounds, of course, not francs?"

"Yes, pounds. I think it was one hundred and fifty, because that is what she left in her will. A hundred and fifty pounds a year to be paid by some trustee or other. If he dies it goes to various charities, but Aunt Emily warned me he might pester me for money."

"And why should he know of your existence?"

"I think he was sent a copy of the will. Aunt Emily would have insisted on that."

Travers nodded. "He wrote to you through the trustees and the letter was sent on. He asked you for the money?"

"Yes. Only just recently though."

Travers held out his hand. "Do you mind if I see the letters?"

"But you can't," she said. "They're horrible. I mean the second one was horrible."

Travers shook his head. "I'm going to ask you a question. Forgive me if I'm being stupid, but has he any actual hold over you yourself?"

She smiled. "Of course not! He was just raking up things against Aunt Emily, and hinting at making trouble."

Travers hooked off his horn-rims again and began giving them another polish.

"Let me get this thing perfectly clear. His letter merely asked for money, and you sent him some—but not as much as he expected."

Her eyes opened. "But, darling, how on earth did you guess that?"

"Because he wouldn't have applied again so quickly," Travers said, "and he wouldn't have begun to put the screw on." He looked up. "You don't consider yourself bound in any way to send him money?"

"I hate him," she said. "I've hated him ever since poor Aunt Emily told me what she did."

"Know anything else about him—his personal appearance and so on?"

She shook her head. "I don't know a thing except what I've told you."

"You've got the address where the money was to be sent?"

She looked through her bag. "Here it is. Hôtel de Sud, Carliens."

"Carliens," said Travers reflectively. "Well past Hyères on the way to Cannes." His fingers went to his glasses again, then fell. "My experience of this sort of thing, and I have had considerable experience in one way or another through the Yard, is that you've got to stop it straight away. May I tell you what I would like to do?"

"But, darling, I want you to tell me."

"Well then. What I think I ought to do is this. I'll leave for my holiday rather earlier and I'll go down to the South, just as I intended, but I'll make it my duty to drop in at the Hôtel du Sud and run, my eye over Uncle Gustave. At my own particular moment I'll have a word or two with him. After that—?" He smiled with a certain grimness and shrugged his shoulders for the rest.

Just before he left for that holiday, Travers thought seriously of ringing Gallois and spending a day or so with him in Paris. To smile at the remembrance of an absent friend is undoubtedly a sign of considerable affection. Gallois had smiled when Charles had mentioned Travers, and now Travers was smiling to himself as he hooked off his glasses and gently polished them. It would be fine to see Gallois again—Gallois in repose, his sad Semitic cast of countenance, the big brooding eyes, the slow and almost shambling gait. Gallois in action—the quick weaving movements of his sensitive fingers, and the voluble flow of his English, which rarely failed for a word and somehow contrived to be more expressive than Travers's own. Gallois, absurdly grateful, prodigiously generous, a showman perhaps and a *poseur*, but only more likeable to those who knew the warmth and genuineness beneath the veneer of flamboyance and assertion.

Yes, thought Travers, it would be good to see Gallois again, but it should be in Paris with Bernice, on the way home. Paris and Gallois were in a way the same thing. Paris was his *milieu*, and it was only there that one saw him, as it were, in full blossoming. And he was an authority On all that the city had of the rare and unusual, the things no tourist saw or was told to see, and Travers nodded to himself as he thought of a day or two in Paris, or perhaps even a week, with Gallois as mentor and guide.

The car was shipped at Folkestone and on that Saturday evening when Gallois finished with the conference at Nîmes, Travers arrived at Aix-en-Provence. He was proposing to revisit all his old haunts along the coast, and early on the Sunday he was through Toulon, and well before lunch had arrived at Furolles. Then all at once he was wondering somewhat amusedly why there should be all the hurry. So he parked the car in the open-air garage of what looked a promising hotel and booked a room for the night.

He had been through Furolles before, but so quickly as never really to have noticed the town, or the countryside, and now he was liking the look of everything. He liked the wooded bastion of hills that sheltered the town from the north. There was a charm and a kind of comfort in the curve of its bay, and something attractive in the sandy stretch that constituted its *plage*.

A gay, colourful town, it looked, and far less cosmopolitan than most, though it was crowded that Sunday with cars that overflowed the municipal park and lined the streets. Perhaps it was usual, he thought, for the district to spend its chief holiday in the little town, and the beach, as he could see, was crowded with sun-bathers, and innumerable heads were bobbing about in the sea.

At lunch he commented on the fact to the waiter.

"But it isn't every Sunday there are so many people," the waiter said. "Everybody comes to-day because of the circus."

"The circus?" said Travers. Every Frenchman, as he knew, loves a circus. "Is it a good one?"

The waiter began to pour out eulogies. The circus had come from Hyères, where he had a friend who had seen it.

It was superb, marvellous, stupendous. There was a troupe of trapeze artists who were very definitely *formidable*. Off went the waiter to attend to other tables, but he was a good waiter and saw that his client was interested, and whenever he came back it was to give some news that he had evidently been gleaning. The Coast was lucky to have the opportunity of seeing a circus of such high class. It was in Italian ownership, and had been in Paris, and now was making its way home by easy stages, which was why one had the good luck to see it at Furolles. The next day it was going to Carliens; indeed, he thought it was staying there for two days at least.

Very near the end of the meal he actually produced some literature which Travers took to the lounge to read over his coffee. The Grand Cirque Pertini was the name. The programme seemed to have the usual constituents, but the interesting thing was that it appeared to have all of them. If everything was there, as the programme announced, then the show was likely to be an uncommonly varied one. There were, for instance, horses with Cossack riders, a star equestrienne, jugglers, performing dogs, a strong man, a boxing kangaroo, the usual clowns, and—billed as the star attraction—the Helmont troupe, trapezists, according to the programme, undoubtedly the most original and daring in the whole world.

"It looks good, this circus of yours," Travers said to the waiter. "It is possible for you to book me a seat?"

"But certainly," the waiter told him. "There are all prices. What would m'sieu wish?"

Travers picked the best seat, a ringside one, at the amazingly cheap price of fifteen francs.

The matinèe was billed as from three o'clock to six, though doubtless it would be over long before. Travers, basing his experience on an intensive acquaintance with French cinemas, guessed also that it would begin a good deal late, and it was almost three o'clock when he left the hotel, but as he made his way to the meadow that lay between the beach and the foothills he found himself one of a dense crowd. All along the coast and even from the village among the hills, people must have been attracted by the fame of that circus, and as the show-ground was neared Travers found himself tightly wedged, yet the perfectly colossal tent was capable of holding them all, if only just. Travers found his seat, and a good one it was. As he squeezed his way along be trod somewhat heavily on the toe of a prosperous-looking, spade-bearded Frenchman, and at once was apologizing profusely. The seat turned out to be next to the Frenchman's and he found he had let himself in for something.

"You are English?" the Frenchman said, in that tongue. When one has the clothes that Travers was wearing, and the face and the accent, there is no particular point in denying it.

"Ago, a good many years, I am in England, for three years," the Frenchman said, and began telling Travers all about Highgate and the perfumery shop in Bond Street. Then happily the band struck up, and while they played Travers was able to be deeply interested in the programme. The species of overture ended, and then just as the Frenchman was beginning again, tumultuous applause announced the entrance of the Ringmaster. He looked something of an Italian, but whatever he was, Travers was unable to follow in its entirety the announcement he was so fervently making. Then at last he was bowing, and as new applause died away in came half a dozen clowns, and on their heels the horses and their Cossack riders.

An hour later when the *entr'acte* arrived, Travers could not help expressing his amazement.

"It is extraordinary," he said in his careful French to his neighbour. "I never saw a circus that was better, and I have seen a good many in my time. It must cost a fortune to run."

The Frenchman shrugged his shoulders and waved a hand at the vast crowded tent.

"There is what you call plenty money, oh? Everywhere they have people like this. Always they are immense and what you call enthusiastic."

"They certainly deserve it," Travers told him. As for enthusiastic, the crowd certainly was that. There was no trouble whatever about getting volunteers for the strong man to hoist above his head, and one local character, with more assurance than discretion, tried a round with the boxing kangaroo and retreated very much the worse for wear, amid laughter time threatened to tear the roof. Then just before the trapezists—the last act and the high-light of the show—came the performing dogs, and the audience fairly rocked in helpless laughter when one of the animals committed a perfectly necessary indiscretion with all that insouciance of which the French, dogs and all, are so gracefully capable.

Off went the dogs, and the laughter died as the Ringmaster began making his last announcement. Except that it was something to do with the act that was to follow Travers understood very little, but the crowd seemed curiously impressed with the importance and even solemnity of the occasion. There was a hush as they awaited the entry of the trapezists, and even the clowns had ceased their antics and had withdrawn in a body to the side of the ring.

But something seemed to have gone wrong. The Ringmaster looked round, then looked again, but more anxiously, and still nothing was happening. He waited for a moment, then made his way out as if to inquire. There was a rustle among the crowd and a murmur of voices, but it was not until another minute that he came back.

"What's he saying?" asked Travers.

"In a minute they come," the Frenchman told him.

But it was another two minutes before a fanfare from the band announced that the trapezists were appearing. The man was slim and of medium height, but the two young women were broad-hipped and compact of build, and the figures of all three had a litheness and an extraordinary grace. All wore white tights, with black masks that completely covered their faces. In the case of the man the whole head was covered, but the hair of the women was visible, and each was a brunette.

"The famous Troupe Helmont," announced Travers's neighbour, still in English and as if he himself was responsible.

"Why are they masked?"

The Frenchman shrugged his shoulders, thought over his English words, then explained in French. There was something mysterious about the artists. Some said this and some said that but he himself believed the rumour that they were Germans and anti-Nazis, who refused to go back to Germany, so that if they revealed their identity it might be dangerous. Travers took a quick look at the programme. The three performers were billed as Jules, Berthe and Jeanne Helmont, and Helmont he rather thought was an Alsatian name.

By slow graceful stages, by rope and trapeze, the women drew themselves up to a platform high in the roof of the tent. Then Jules bowed and also slowly drew himself up by the hanging rope. The muscles rippled as hand rose effortlessly over hand, and when at last he reached his platform the crowd could not keep back a cheer.

Then as he stood there, wiping his hands, an attendant came in, a tiny cage in his hand. He stopped at the foot of the rope, opened the cage, and out came a little white rat. The crowd gaped, and then as the attendant stopped almost to the ground, and with one hand grasped the rope and made it taut, the voice of Jules came from high up in the roof. What he really called Travers could not quite catch, but it sounded like, "*Viens, Auguste, viens!*"

Auguste came. Before Travers was aware he was running up the rope. For a moment he was lost against a white section of the canvas and then all at once there was a "Hoop-là!" and there he was on the shoulder of Jules and the crowd was roaring.

As for the actual performance Travers had seen nothing more graceful, more rhythmic, or more exquisitely timed. There were moments when he was afraid to look as a figure flashed in a swallow-dive across the height of that roof, and it was only when the shout of the crowd announced a safety and some new perfection of finish that he would venture to look up again. The amazing thing was that all the time Auguste—the little white rat—crouched on the shoulders of Jules and hurtled with him backwards and forwards across the terrifying space.

The last hair-raising somersaults were made and down the trapezists came, and bowed and bowed to the deafening applause. But Auguste was not there. Apparently for him a special and personal descent was being reserved. In came the attendant to steady the rope. Jules snapped his fingers and looked upwards, and there was Auguste beginning the downward trip. Into his little cage he went, the attendant raised it and bowed, and the applause and laughter were the most tremendous of the day.

Out blared the band again, round the ring went the clowns, and the whole crowd rose to its feet as the canvases were whipped back to make a score of new exits. Travers stayed on for a moment till the first rush should be over, then caught up with his neighbour again. The Frenchman glanced back at him over his shoulder.

"It was good, the circus?"

"Very good indeed," Travers told him in English. "I wouldn't have missed it for anything. They were superb, those artists."

"In London you do not see like them, no?"

Travers smiled and shook his head. What he was thinking was that, marvellous and even uncanny as the Helmont troupe had been, it was Auguste who had really stolen the show.

CHAPTER III
AUGUSTE IS TEMPERAMENTAL

AFTER BREAKFAST on the Monday morning, Travers began thinking out the preliminaries of his campaign against Gustave Rionne. What he decided was that he would put up at some other Carliens hotel, and then find the whereabouts of the Hôtel du Sud. Practically every hotel was open to non-residents, so he could probably have a meal there, chat with the waiter and ultimately have a look at Rionne. As for the rest there was no particular hurry. The main thing was to get some definite impression of the precise kind of scoundrel the man was.

It was quite early when he started out on that short journey of twenty kilometres. About half-way to Carliens, the now ageing, but still highly efficient, Rolls was overtaken by that very *autobus* in which Gallois was sitting. The Hôtel de France was recommended to Gallois by the conductor of the *autobus*, but Travers had to use his own judgment. Finally he chose the Hôtel Royal, where he was shown a charming room that overlooked the pines and sea.

Carliens was many times the size of Furolles, but for a holiday Travers would have chosen the smaller place every time. Carliens was modern and the least bit raucous. If Furolles was a water-colour, then Carliens was a particularly gaudy poster. It had a dozen fine hotels, mostly white and new; its beach, seen from the hotel window, was a patchwork of sun umbrellas, brilliant roofed bathing-sheds and huts and shining kiosks. Even the trim palms that lined the too spotless front seemed somehow new, and when he looked back from the quiet hills he was irresistibly reminded of Brighton.

It was eleven o'clock when he came out to the street in a brilliant sun and what was still left of the morning cool. As he made his way to the office of the local Syndicat d'Initiative he had some personal evidence of the up-to-dateness of the place, when ahead of him he saw a man levelling a camera. Travers spotted what he was at once. He looked quite a youngish fellow, in spite of his natty imperial, and he gave a charming smile as he handed the card. Travers, rarely impatient of his fellow men, smiled too as he took it, and a few yards on he read it. The card was actually printed in five languages: French, English, German, Italian, and Dutch, and the English version read:

JAQUES LEBRUN
SPECIALIST IN EVERY KIND OF PHOTOGRAPHY
INFORMS YOU THAT THIS PHOTOGRAPH OF YOU CAN
BE SEEN AT 10, RUE DES ALPES
AT EXACTLY ONE HOUR FROM NOW

Not only that: there was a neat little map, showing exactly how to arrive at the Rue des Alpes. Travers had to smile again. Monsieur Lebrun certainly deserved to get on.

At the Syndicat d'Initiative Travers was given local and district maps and guides and was patiently shown the precise whereabouts of the Hôtel du Sud. It was in what was called the old town at the far end of the beach, so Travers walked back beneath the palms along the fine new road that skirted the bay, and he passed within twenty yards of the chair in which at that moment Gallois was lolling at his ease. A moment or two and he came across another unusual specimen of modernity and a not unamusing one, which was a new public lavatory obviously for the use of bathers and reserved for men. But it was not of the usual type—the iron surround with even the knees of its users visible—but a long, if narrow, wholly covered-in affair with porcelain walls, running water and chromium-plated metal work. There were also four closets with automatic entry on deposit of a franc. Travers, always insatiably curious, invested that sum for the sake of a look inside. The whole thing he decided would have been a credit to any municipality. But, as he amusedly assured himself, none too well patronized, for the beach was fairly well crowded and his inspection had taken the best part of five minutes, and the fine new lavatory had been used only by one small boy, and he obviously English.

At the kiosk he bought a paper and read to pass the time till well after noon. It took no more than a couple of minutes to find the Hôtel du Sud, but when he saw it, he had something of a shock. It was very small, and very frowsty, and yet, as he knew, its looks might belie it. It might be one of those unpretentious places known only to the initiated, with fine cooking of the country and a cellar as good as the best. But the menu in the window gave no promise of that. Lunch was twelve francs, wine included, and the choice as uninspiring as he had ever seen.

So strong a physical repulsion was he feeling to the place that he had to screw up his courage to the point of entering. A waiter pounced on him at once and ushered him into a dining-room—a tiny affair that looked over the road. There were about eight tables and only one occupied, by a family of obvious provincials, consisting of father, mother and two boys.

"You have rooms here?" Travers asked the waiter.

"Yes," he said, "but they are all occupied."

"There are several rooms?"

The waiter shrugged his shoulders. Four rooms only, he said, and exhibited the menu. Travers ordered a different wine and sat down to lunch. The seat he had chosen had its back to the door, and facing him, slightly sideways, was a mirror. A young couple entered, and then, as Travers judged from the manner of the waiter, an elderly man who was certainly a guest. In the mirror Travers studied him carefully. He looked the professional type, if somewhat down at heel. He was of medium height, spare in build, with a head that was almost white and a head entirely bald. There was something supercilious in the way he looked round at his fellow feeders as if he found his environment beneath him, and did not trouble a couple of sous who knew it. But he had no quarrel with his food, for he ate quickly and noisily, napkin tucked well into his collar, and he had no time whatever for talk.

Travers, making his meal deliberately leisurely, watched the room through the mirror. The complement of four rooms of residents was completed, and another table was taken by three young men. They were talking about the circus. Then the table with the two boys and their parents began talking about the circus too. They were going to the afternoon performance and the boys seemed particularly interested in the boxing kangaroo and Auguste, the little white rat.

Travers had just finished wrestling with the incredibly underdone beef when the elderly man gave a final gasp as of satisfaction and repletion, and rose from the table. Travers continued his own meal at the same methodical pace. When it was over he ordered a *café-filtre* and writing-materials, then at long last he was alone in the room with the waiter and about to pay the bill.

"I should have met a gentleman here," he said. "A stranger of the name of Laroche, who should have introduced himself."

"And he did not come?"

"Apparently not," Travers said. "I suppose, by chance, he could not have been the gentleman who was sitting at that table there?"

"But no," the waiter told him promptly, "That is M. Rionne, who is residing here."

"Well, perhaps there is some mistake, and this M. Laroche will turn up to-morrow."

Then he had a sudden idea; and it was quite a large note that he offered in payment of the bill. No sooner had the waiter gone for change than he was pocketing the menu which had been used by Rionne and bore his fingerprints. And the idea was also part of another one, for when, he came out to the street again he consulted his map and then made his way to the headquarters of the police.

There he stated he had come about a matter in which he desired the assistance of the police, though he preferred to disclose it only to someone in authority. Then his particulars were taken, his passport examined, and he was asked about references. Travers quoted Gallois, then was asked to wait in a private room. In ten minutes a sergeant of police came in and Travers was of the opinion that the ten minutes had been employed in inquiries at the Hôtel Royal. In any case the sergeant's manner was most cordial. His name was Fournal, he said, and once he had actually met the famous Gallois.

"*Voilà un homme formidable*," he said with a shake of the head, and Travers gave a nod of earnest agreement. Then the explanations were made and in strict confidence.

"You yourself, then, propose to approach this Rionne," Fournal summarized, "and to inform him that if he continues these efforts to obtain money from your wife you will refer matters to us, and you therefore warn us beforehand."

"Yes," said Travers, "But I would also like you to do this. Find out at once, and through Inspector Gallois if you wish, whether Rionne has a criminal record in France. That should give me a considerable hold over him when I actually decide to speak."

Fournal twirled his moustache. That, he said, could be arranged, but first it might be as well to endeavour to obtain his fingerprints.

Travels produced the menu and again explained.

"Ah!" said Fournal delightedly, and the gasp, Travers was to learn later, was a mannerism he had learned from one of his superiors. "When one is a detective one has all the tricks."

"And how soon will there be a reply?" Travers wanted to know.

Fournal looked at his own watch, then at the clock in the tower of the Hôtel de Ville. Paris could be rung immediately and the prints could be hurried to Toulon to catch the afternoon 'plane. Probably before midnight therefore an answer might be obtained over the 'phone.

Once more Travers was very well satisfied. It was still short of three o'clock when his glance happened to turn northwards, behind the massed villas of the foothills to the higher hills and their shaded, pine-covered slopes. Ten minutes later he was clear of the last of the villas and still making his way upwards, with the heavy smell of the pines about him and the unmistakable scent of wild thyme.

At about half-past three he was well up in the hills, and, in spite of the shade, tremendously hot. So he rested on a carpet of pine needles, his back against a tree. A minute or two and he was nodding, and then, with some last instinct for comfort, he turned on his side and was lying at full length when he fell asleep.

It was an hour later when he awoke, blinked, and slowly raised himself. So comfortable was he in that scented warmth that his first thought was to lie down again. Then he looked at his watch and got to his feet. A few steps and he was on the narrow rocky track which would bring him down to the fork, but as he stepped from the bank he heard the harsh grinding of a car and almost at once he saw it, and its driver stopped at the sight of him.

It was a rather old saloon and the driver was a man of about thirty clean-shaven and well spoken, though now there was a definite petulance in his tone.

"*Pardon,* m'sieur, but is this the road for Lizou?"

"Lizou?" Travers remembered. "I imagine you ought to have taken the right turn at the fork."

The other shrugged his shoulders exasperatedly. There was no indication, he said, and he had taken the left, and then it had petered out into that abominable track.

Travers was sympathetic and consolatory and admitted that he had done the same thing himself. Then he produced the map of the district and showed precisely where they were at that moment.

"A thousand thanks," the man said. "All that is necessary then is to reverse."

More thanks, and the reversing began. Travers followed and was just in time to catch a glimpse of the car as it moved behind the pines on what was the main road to Lizou. A minute or two later he heard the sound of a bell. It was the clock in the Hôtel de Ville striking five, and with a sudden thirst upon him he quickened his pace. What had taken half an hour to climb took barely a quarter to descend. The clock on the Hôtel de Ville struck a quarter past the hour as he took a seat beneath the shaded awning of a café-restaurant on the front and wiped his brow and his sticky collar. A large *café-crème* was ordered, and when he had drunk it he looked round to order a second.

It was at that moment that the shouting came. It was a yell, sudden and startling. A man was in the road about a hundred yards to the right, just in front of that beach lavatory. What he was calling, Travers had no idea, but he was also waving and beckoning. Then in the same moment a gendarme was making for him at the double. But others had understood what the frantic man had called, for people around Travers were on their feet and others were moving. More people were on the pavement and they were running. Travers, half knocked off his feet by two men who thrust by him, calmly sat down again.

As for the man in the street, he could no longer be seen, for from pavement to pavement there was a crowd, and still more of the curious were making their way from the beach and the road.

One of the waiters had run across. Within a minute he was coming back.

"What is it?" Travels asked.

"Who knows?" He shrugged his shoulders philosophically. "Some say a man was stabbed; perhaps there was a fight."

More gendarmes appeared and the crowd was being pushed back from the immediate vicinity of the lavatory. Then a car flashed by and in it Travers caught a glimpse of his friend Fournal. Travers was on his feet at once. When Fournal left the car he was at his heels. A way was made through the crowd, and Travers still followed, like one having authority. At the very entrance to the lavatory Fournal happened to glance back.

"Ah—M. Travers!" he said, and then the surprise became interrogation. "You are concerned in this? A witness perhaps?"

Travers smiled and shook his head. The noise of the crowd was so great that Fournal had to shout, and before Travers could speak he was bellowing furiously. More gendarmes must be fetched, and the road roped off. It was impossible to work in such a clamour. Then he let out a roar at the crowd itself. Every one was to go. It was forbidden to remain on pain of arrest.

There was slightly less noise as the half-dozen gendarmes sprang into action; then he turned to Travers with a look that seemed to expect some word of approbation. But Travers was staring, and in a moment Fournal was staring too. Between a couple of protesting gendarmes, a tall figure was making his placid way. Travers blinked, and his fingers went nervously to his glasses.

It was not much after ten o'clock when Gallois arrived at Carliens that Monday morning, and when he had seen his room and had a brief gossip with Monsieur Velot, the proprietor, and his wife, he wondered what he could do with himself till lunch. But first he took a stroll through the main shopping street, and almost at once an immense poster caught his eye. The Grand Cirque Pertini had arrived. Gallois took a look round as if to make sure that no one who knew him should catch him in anything so frivolous, then he read the poster from top to bottom. A supplementary bill announced that the circus was staying for three days and there would be five performances: two on the Monday, two on the Tuesday and one on the Wednesday.

The eyes of Gallois left the poster, and it was a queer reflective look that he was casting up at the sky. Bariche had been in his thoughts as he left the hotel, and now he was remembering something, Bariche had been mad about circuses. On two occasions, as the authorities were aware, he had actually met his future victim at a circus, and in his patient examination of all the vague and tenuous evidence that had subsequently been amassed, Gallois had more than once had the curious feeling—a feeling which he did not impart even to Charles— that the career of Bariche, and the man himself, stood out in their vagueness against some stronger background of the circus and its file.

Then he was shaking his head. His eyes fell on the poster again, and though he nodded benignly he was not prepared to admit, even to himself, that the circus was an attraction. But at least the poster made him turn back towards the hotel. In the open garage at the back was a pile of canvas chairs for the use of guests, and he carried one across the road to the beach and sat in the sun as he had promised himself, with his mind on the seventeenth-century dramatists. Then his eyes began to wander to the bathers, and there was another distraction as the photographer moved along the beach, snapping this group and that and handing out his cards. As he came his way Gallois pretended to nap, and when he had gone the desire for work had gone too and he lay back in his chair, watching the divers and the romping children. So quickly did the morning pass that hunger told him it was well past noon.

M. Velot and his wife were both at the desk as he came in, and he lingered for a brief gossip. There was a regret that he was staying only until Wednesday.

"Fortunately you will not miss the circus," Velot said.

Gallois smiled sadly. "I am too old for circuses."

"But no!" protested Madame.

"It is unique," added Velot. "My nephew who saw it yesterday at Furolles says it is unbelievable."

"To go to such things one needs a companion," Gallois said.

Velot shrugged his shoulders and smiled. "Come with me then. I'm going this afternoon. Would you like me to buy you a ticket when I buy my own?"

So just before three o'clock Gallois was in a seat at the circus, and, though one would scarcely have judged it from his face, was enjoying himself immensely. As he explained to Velot, in the course of a sudden argument, it was the perfection of artistry which he himself, as something of an artist, could appreciate.

The show went on until the final item had arrived. The crowd was not so large as at Furolles, because perhaps Carliens knew it had the choice of performances, but it was enthusiastic enough, and there was the same curiously dramatic hush before the entrance of the trio for their aerial act. There was also once more a delay, but this time there was no hitch. It was, one might have gathered, a calculated delay by the management to increase suspense and whet the appetite.

"They tell me these trapezists are masked," Velot said. "The man, I believe, is a Russian prince, a cousin of the late Tsar, and one of the women is his wife."

"These cousins of the Tsar could populate a province," Gallois remarked dryly. Then there was a blare from the band and the trapezists entered to a vast burst of applause. While they were climbing to their lofty platforms, Velot whispered again.

"Ah! Now we see the rat!"

Gallois raised his eyebrows. Velot explained. "There is a rat called Auguste, who's also going to climb the rope and perform. But, *voilà!*"

An attendant had come in with the cage. He scooped and held the rope taut. The cage door was opened, Jules called from high in the roof and at once the rat began to climb. Then something went wrong. All at once Auguste scampered down and shot back into his cage. The attendant picked him out and placed him at the rope once more.

Jules called. The rat refused to budge.

"That's strange," said Velot. "My nephew said that yesterday he was perfect."

"The rat perhaps is a woman and temperamental," said Gallois, with his same dry smile.

But the Ringmaster was calling something. The cage door was shut and Auguste was taken off. Then came the announcement. Auguste had not been well that morning, but the Ringmaster promised that everything should be done to ensure his performance that night. Also with many grandiloquent gestures and flourishes he assured the audience that even without Auguste they were about to see something that they would always remember.

"The gentleman has a considerable gift of explanation," whispered Gallois.

But when the act was over his applause was as loud as any one's.

"For my part," he told Velot, as they were making their way out, "the others can have this Auguste. I am not one of those who desire to see the artistic and the superb mixed up with buffoonery."

The two were wedged in the crowd that made its way out along the narrow lane to the main road. Very far from all of the population had patronized the circus, for Gallois, peering over the hats of those ahead of him, could see a crowd near the hotel and there seemed to be gendarmes who were keeping them in order. At that moment a young man in a bathing-costume came running from that way along the beach and he caught sight of Velot. It was the nephew, and he called excitedly across, gesticulating back at the crowd in the road ahead.

"Murder! A man stabbed!"

There was a swaying as the circus crowd heard the words. Some pulled up to hear more, some started to run ahead, and in the mix-up Gallois had gone before Velot was aware of it, and had slipped deftly through the edge of the crowd. Where others ran his long legs strode.

Another minute and he had slipped through a momentary gap where the gendarmes were forcing back the crowd. Two of them made to stop him, but he waved a bland hand and went on. Then he stared and his mouth gaped. He halted a second, then his face was beaming, and he was moving forward with hand outstretched.

CHAPTER IV
A SHOCK FOR CHARLES

"MY FRIEND, it is really you?" Gallois was beginning, as it were, where he had left off, for with Travers he would never speak anything but English. And there was more in it than the opportunity to practise his remarkable knowledge of the language. It was a proud assertion of a profound respect for things English, and the outward and audible sign of something that was more than friendship for Travers himself.

Travers grasped the hand. Fournal was still staring.

"It is M. Gallois!"

"And why not?" asked Gallois blandly.

"But, m'sieu, only two hours ago I was assured by Paris that you were in Nîmes."

The eyes of Gallois narrowed. There was news then about Bariche.

"You had some information for me?"

"It was M. Travers who desired the information."

Gallois looked, gasped, and shrugged his shoulders in humorous despair.

"Apparently there is a mystery. And you, my friend, what is your name?"

Fournal told him.

"Then, my dear Fournal, why are the three of us here at this excellent public lavatory?"

"Ah!" said Fournal and whipped round. The two followed.

On the floor of that brave new lavatory lay a man face downwards, a knife neatly in his back. Further on by the closets was another man, a civilian, standing by a gendarme. He was trying to attract the attention of Fournal, who was trying hard not to see him.

"Well, what happened?" Fournal demanded of the gendarme.

"It is M. Croize who knows," the gendarme told him.

Then Fournal condescended to be aware of the witness, Georges Croize, a local chemist, whose story was simplicity itself, had entered the lavatory in time to see the final agonies of the dead man, then he had run out and summoned the police.

"You saw no one else in here?" demanded Fournal.

"Not a soul," Croize assured him.

"You have touched nothing—the knife, for instance?"

Before Croize could reply Fournal felt a hand on his arm. Travers was blinking away in considerable perturbation.

"M. Fournal, I know this man," he was saying. "It is M. Rionne."

Fournal gasped. "The man about whom you inquired?"

"Yes," said Travers.

Fournal stared again, then snapped an order. The gendarme was to fetch from the Hôtel du Sud someone capable of identifying the deceased. He turned to see Gallois, who had been stooping to examine the handle of the knife, getting to his feet again and with a shake of his head.

"There are no prints?"

"None that are visible," Gallois told him. "Is it permitted to ask exactly who he is?"

Travers began explaining in English. Fournal, for some reason known only to himself, began examining the soles of the dead man's boots, and then was wriggling his fingers under the coat to feel in the inner pockets.

Something was in a breast-pocket and he hoisted the body and felt again. Out came two letters, each in an envelope that bore the dead man's name and the Hôtel du Sud address. One was an ordinary bank form, which, as Travers explained, had been enclosed with the last quarter's instalment of the pension. The second letter was actually that which had been sent by Bernice. That too, Travers explained, and translated. Then feet were heard outside, and in came the waiter of the Hôtel du Sud. The proprietor, it appeared, was out.

"The name of this man, please?" Fournal demanded officially.

"It is M. Rionne who resides at the hotel."

"And how long has he been at the hotel?"

The waiter thought, counted on his fingers, then made it five weeks.

Fournal's questions thereupon seemed exhausted and he turned with a shrug of his shoulders to Gallois.

"He had friends?" asked Gallois.

"Not that I knew of, m'sieu."

"And did he ever talk over his business with you?"

"No, m'sieu."

"That surprises me little," said Gallois dryly. "But did he always remain in his room at the hotel?"

"Sometimes, m'sieu, but if it was fine he would take a walk."

"Ah!" said Gallois. "Now we're getting somewhere. And where did he walk?"

The waiter explained that he had no idea. What perhaps he should have said was that the gentleman went out. It was his own personal opinion that he had a walk.

Gallois sighed and waved a hand at Fournal to indicate that the witness was once again his.

Fournal simply sent him off with the flea of the law in his ear. There was to be no talking about what he had seen and he must hold himself in readiness to be questioned further by the authorities. Travers had the idea that the blustering was merely to make time, and in truth there seemed precious little that Fournal or any one else could do. Fournal himself was realizing as much, but he looked profoundly wise for a moment or two, examined the body again, and then the mountain, having been in that much labour, produced the following conversational mouse.

"I find it strange, this crime."

"On the contrary," Gallois told him. "A man of the type of this Rionne always has enemies."

"Precisely," said Fournal promptly. "And it was such a one who attacked him here?"

"Attacked!"

"But yes!"

Gallois shrugged his shoulders. "When you raised the body you doubtless saw his clothes at the same time. You observed, for instance, that he was in the act of urinating when the assassin came in. This assassin wore rubber soles or *espadrilles,* and before Rionne could turn his head, the knife was in his back. That, I think, is not attack. On the contrary it is simply assassination."

"And the assassin?" asked Fournal.

"Who knows? Even before Rionne fell he had gone. One step and he was on the pavement, and on the pavement he was unobserved."

Fournal nodded respectfully. "All that is undoubtedly true, and you advise what?"

Gallois looked surprised. "It is not for me to advise. But haven't I already been told that you are inquiring into his history? Very well; out of that there ought to arrive a motive which will lead you to the assassin. There will also doubtless be a search of his room, and the assistance of the newspapers. And, since he seems to have been secretive about his affairs, why not photograph the face at once and display it everywhere, with a request for information? By that you may learn where he spent his time when he was not in the hotel."

Fournal whipped out his note-book, but Gallois was holding out his hand. "If we can be of service, do not hesitate to call on us at the Hôtel de France."

Fournal stared blankly. "You leave then, m'sieu?"

"We also have business that is not unimportant," Gallois told him enigmatically.

Fournal followed them both to the exit, and saw a way cleared. To avoid the crowd Gallois cut through a kind of alley and almost at once was in the hotel yard. Half an hour later Travers had changed his quarters and he had heard all about Bariche and that rendezvous of the Wednesday afternoon.

Dinner began at seven o'clock. Gallois and Travers had a preliminary apéritif on the veranda and the conversation turned on coincidences with special reference to Rionne. Gallois rounded off the discussion with something of amused contempt. The *affaire Rionne* was one which might have been specially arranged to suit the brains of Fournal.

"An excellent man," he hastened to add in his fluent English, "but without finesse. He is of the type that fills in documents in a handwriting that is superb, and after that—" He shrugged his shoulders, and then his expression changed and he was getting to his feet, for Fournal himself was coming in.

"Messieurs," he said and bowed. "M. Velot said I should find you here."

A sheet of paper was being placed ceremoniously on the table.

"This is the record of Rionne received from Paris. The fingerprints have not yet arrived, but there is no doubt that it is the same man."

The record was a peculiar one. Rionne had first come under the notice of the police under his own name in 1920, when charged at Enghien with causing an abortion. He had been fined five thousand francs with imprisonment for two years. After that he had disappeared till 1933, when defendant in an action brought by a patient for injuries caused by his carelessness in a skin-grafting operation. That was in Luxembourg, where it turned out he had been practising for nine years under the name of Casimir Dufont. After his expulsion from the Principality he was heard of as recently as the previous February, when under his own name he was expelled from Switzerland for suspected complicity in drug trafficking. He had to resume his own name, Travers explained, because of the terms of the will.

Fournal pompously produced from his pocket a copy of the will and other papers found in the dead man's room at the hotel. There were medical diplomas, for instance, and even a bundle of letters from grateful patients, but nothing to indicate the identity of a possible assassin.

"You have a public museum here?" Gallois asked jocularly. "If so, here are some excellent exhibits. Meanwhile the inquiry progresses?"

Fournal said that M. Aumade, the local examining magistrate, was already employed about the case, and he requested a visit by M. Travers at ten o'clock the next morning at the Hôtel de Ville. He would also be honoured to meet Inspector Gallois.

"Give him our compliments," Gallois told him largely, "and say that without fail we shall be there."

But he seemed sardonically amused when Fournal had gone.

"This Rionne is what you call a fleabite; he is not worth the trouble of an inquiry. M. Aumade discovers the assassin perhaps, who is some associate of Rionne in Switzerland and whom he has, as you say, double-crossed. Even then, what does it matter? You and I do not concern ourselves with affairs so trivial. In courtesy we call on this M. Aumade, and after that—? *Eh bien,* we await the afternoon of Wednesday, which promises a real occasion."

The second gong had long since sounded and he got to his feet.

"As far as I am concerned," Travers said, "I am of your own and Dogberry's opinion."

"Dogberry?"

Travers explained.

"You will pardon if I make a note," Gallois said delightedly. "At the moment, I also occupy myself with Shakespeare. And what was the opinion of this excellent Dogberry?"

Travers gave it in French. Gallois chuckled enormously.

"'He thanked God he had disembarrassed himself of a rogue.' And you also, my friend, and Madame your wife, have disembarrassed yourselves of a rogue. That makes the epitaph of this Rionne. The quotation, if you will excuse me, was superb. Sometime I shall also avail myself of it."

After dinner the talk turned to the Wednesday, and Travers ventured to remark that the Bariche affair might turn out to be something quite simple too. If the priest turned up and the information was given, the arrest of Bariche would follow and that was that. There would be, for instance, no thrill of a hunt.

"It is nothing then that I should be able to vindicate myself?" asked Gallois with a reproachful sadness.

"But of course," Travers told him. "After what you have told me I shall be delighted."

The eyes of Gallois narrowed. "For my part, when I lay my hand upon this Bariche, it will be on a man who lives and has blood in his veins. To me this Bariche has been words on paper, and a heap, like this, of documents." His lips curled in infinite disgust. "The Bariche of documents, the Bariche of what you call second-hand, as he is described to me by witnesses, who are mostly fools."

Travers could not quite understand the last remark. Gallois explained it at some length. Bariche had not chosen his victims from the lower and less educated classes like Landru. Those were the classes that came forward at once to the police if they suspected a relative had been a victim; but the victims of Bariche appeared to have been of a superior class, whose relatives would do everything to avoid publicity. From these there were doubtlessly a dozen individuals who guessed that some daughter or female relative had been a Bariche victim, but who would never come forward with information to the police and so risk scandal in their own localities, and most of the information the police did possess had come only from the Auteuil fire and chance revelations arising out of it. There had also been third-party, or anonymous, communications by people not relatives of the victim. Those people had been the nosy-parkers and scandalmongers, who, when the Bariche affair first blazed out, suspected that the excuses given by relatives for the absence or disappearance of someone was not as genuine as it seemed, and that the someone might indeed be a victim of the new Bluebeard.

Travers raised his glass. "Well, here's luck on Wednesday and hoping your priest turns up." Then he was smiling and shaking his head. "I wonder if you will pardon me—I should say, understand me—if I put forward a point of view. Do you know what I think would be the ideal thing? That on Wednesday you should receive information which would allow you definitely to convince your superiors that Bariche is alive, but that you should not be able to lay your hands on him."

"You mean that he should escape?"

"Wait a moment," Travers said. "I don't know that I did mean that, but let him escape if you like. Anything provided you do not see him before you ultimately lay your hands on him. Think of the thrill you'll have in being absolutely certain Bariche is somewhere and not knowing who he really is. That waiter there, for instance, might be Bariche, or that man just coming in—the lame man with the black beard. You might even sit down with Bariche at the same table and not know him."

Gallois shook his head. "There are times, my friend, when I might enjoy a sensation of the kind, but in the case of this Bariche—no." His eyes turned dreamily away and he was smiling with an infinite sadness. "What you call the thrill will come for me when I approach my superiors and I say: 'Permit me to present M. Bariche, who was dead, but by some drollery has decided to come alive again.'"

After dinner Velot, who loved a gossip, made a third with them, and later Madame joined them. It was getting pretty late when in came a resident who was a stranger to Gallois.

"The circus was good?" Velot called to him.

"It was superb."

"And Auguste? He had recovered from his indisposition?"

Auguste also was superb, he was told. Then Gallois had to admit to Travers that Velot had dragged him to the circus and Madame was announcing that, after all she had heard, she would certainly go to the next day's matinée. Then at last Travers and Gallois made a move for bed.

"Before I forget it," said Travers as they went along the corridor. "Might I be somewhere on hand on Wednesday? I've plenty of time to spare, so if you like I'll drive you to Toulon in the car. It will be nice to see Charles again too."

Gallois said he would be delighted to accept the offer and Charles would be delighted to see Travers, of whom he was an admirer.

Travers smiled. "I wonder what he's actually doing in Nîmes, while you're away?"

The smile of Gallois was almost a chuckle. "Whatever he does, my friend, there is one thing of which we are certain. It is not the museums or the antiquities with which he occupies himself."

But what Charles was actually doing at that very moment was nothing at all, at least, actively; and what he was doing passively, so to speak, would never have been guessed in a hundred attempts by either Gallois or Travers. The nearest they might have come at it would have been to say that he was in bed. As a matter of fact Charles, at the moment, was within eight kilometres of Carliens, lying unconscious on a bed, and in his head was a wound in which there had been put no less than twelve stitches.

How it came about was this. Charles contrived after all to be in a position to leave Nîmes on the Sunday night, though he had intended going on the Monday morning, which would ensure his not running up against Gallois, for whose discipline he had the profoundest respect. But at that conference at Nîmes he had become friendly with the son of a certain dignitary at Toulon and as this son was returning to Toulon late on the Sunday night, Charles accepted his offer of a ride.

Now he had always had a hankering after things mechanical. He might indeed have been described as a born driver, with work and Paris giving him few chances of driving. During the journey that Sunday night an idea had come to him to spend his two days in touring the countryside. But first he got into touch with the Toulon police, in order to make sure that there was definitely no more news about the priest, and from them he learned that Gallois was in Carliens.

He then hired an old, but quite serviceable, two-seater from the garage, to be returned in two days' time, and late that Monday afternoon he set off for Hyères. Near the town he looked out for a kind of by-pass short cut, which his friend had told him would avoid the suburbs, and bring him out farther along the coast road. He found it, as he thought, but in any case it was a glorious evening, the car was going well and he was in his element. Then he began looking to the right for a sight of the sea, and was puzzled that no sea was in sight, and soon he knew he must be on the wrong road and with no map.

So he waited at the cross-roads till a passing motorist advised him to go on to Gevrol-les-Vignes. Five kilometres short of the town he had a nasty puncture and found when he had fixed on the spare that he had no pump with which to blow it up. Dusk was already in the sky before another motorist came to his help. Happily the car lights functioned well and then at a fork he took what was obviously the road to Gevrol, only to be on the wrong one. When he saw the lights ahead and imagined them to be those of Gevrol they were only the lights of Lizou.

The descent was steep and the road still rough from the spring rains, and exceedingly tortuous. Then when he was on the outskirts of the tiny town and the precipice that had been to his right had shrunk to a mere slope, a huge *camion* came suddenly hurtling round the bend. Its lights were in his eyes and at once it seemed to be on top of him. As he wrenched his steering-wheel right, it caught his bumper and pitched him to a gap in the broken-down stone wall. Without pausing, the *camion* roared on. The car trembled for a moment on the edge, struck the fallen stones again, then toppled down the slope.

But at the foot of the slope on a plateau that ran alongside the gorge was a cottage occupied by a roadman who at the moment was absent. On his return two hours later he found the car in his garden and the unconscious Charles in it. A hundred yards away was the nearest house, which was that of a Dr. Debran. That, as far as Charles was concerned, was fortunate. The doctor had been in the Colonial service and was still a sufferer from recurrent malaria. That Monday night he anticipated an attack and was already dosing himself with quinine. If the accident had taken place a day later he would have been unable perhaps to stitch the cut in the skull, though Gabrielle, his sister, would certainly have attempted it herself.

Beyond dents and minor breakages the car sustained practically no damage at all. Altogether then it was what one might call a remarkably lucky accident for Charles. If—as Gallois was later forced to wonder—it was an accident at all.

CHAPTER V
AT THE RENDEZVOUS

M. AUMADE, the examining magistrate who was undertaking the inquiry into the murder of Rionne, was a man of charm and affability, and Gallois was to be impressed by his industry and talent. He saw the two in his private room where Gallois introduced Travers, much to that gentleman's embarrassment, not only as a friend but a famous expert of Scotland Yard.

M. Aumade expressed himself as doubly honoured. With so much talent, he said, they should soon arrive at the murderer of Rionne. There might even have been a twinkle in his eye as he added: "There is also cur excellent confrere Fournal, who, I believe, is known to you."

Gallois permitted himself a smile. "The excellent Fournal will stay with you. As for us, unhappily, we must both leave to-morrow."

"A matter of urgency?" Aumade asked regretfully.

"Yes," Gallois said. "An affair which I regret at the moment I am unable to confide to you."

"Well, there may be time yet," Aumade said confidently. "But first of all some rather boring business must be settled."

What he immediately wanted was a complete official statement by Travers. Among other things the English trustees of the will would have to be notified of the death of Rionne. But it was all tedious work and it was not until an hour later that Aumade was asking Gallois if he had formed any new opinions about the murder.

Gallois asked if he might speak frankly.

"We have almost a complete history of the man," he said, "thanks to the statement of M. Travers, and his record. He committed some professional crime and left England probably to avoid arrest, but resumed practice in Luxembourg where we imagine him going more and more down the social ladder until even his professional skill is impaired and he bungles a case. Then he goes to Switzerland, from where he is forced to request money from his former wife. Even though he obtains it he becomes an associate of drug pedlars and perverts. He is expelled from there, and now, almost at once, we find him here." He gave a shrug of his shoulders. "What then should we conclude?"

Aumade pulled a wry face. "These are many things one could conclude. Your own deductions are—What?"

Gallois shrugged his shoulders again. "That he arrived here with all the secrets of the gang. In their opinion it was dangerous for him to retain those secrets. Someone or other was sent from Switzerland and—*voilà!*"

"The secret then of this murder lies in Switzerland?"

Gallois smiled warily. "The discovery of the assassin may depend on the co-operation of the Swiss police."

Aumade smiled. "That, I can assure you, has already been sought." Then he was giving a shrewd look. "May I put a question which seems to me somewhat pertinent? There was nothing taken from his room. Why remove the man when something which is a danger may remain written down on paper?"

The eyes of Gallois narrowed as if in pain. He was loath to admit that he had spoken quickly and without sufficient thought.

"May I make a suggestion?" Travers said.

"Suggestions are what we wish," Aumade told him.

"Then the chemist, Croize, entered the lavatory in time to see the agonies of Rionne. Therefore he arrived within some seconds of the knife thrust. Within those seconds the assassin left the lavatory, after a precautionary peep outside, and was walking along the beach. He would not even have run or he would have attracted attention, so we must imagine that he walked, and if anything at a slightly sub-normal pace. At once, and this is the important point as I see it, Croize was in the road and shouting. The murderer knew the alarm had been given, for he must have still been within earshot—also, as far as he knew, the man who was raising the alarm might be acquainted with Rionne, and therefore the murderer was afraid to go to the hotel as he had originally intended."

Aumade had been slowly nodding an agreement, but he had a last question to put.

"But the pockets of the dead man?"

"Admitted," said Travers. "We know what was left but we do not know what was taken."

Gallois cut in. "What is being done in addition to Switzerland?"

"First, at the very excellent suggestion of our good friend Fournal, we are at this moment posting up photographs of the dead man in the town and district and requesting information. It is possible that the Swiss associate who murdered him may even have been seen in his company."

"An excellent idea," said Gallois dryly. "An idea in fact which I should have been happy to have thought of myself."

It was nearly noon when they left the Hôtel de Ville. Travers suggested a brief walk along the front for the sake of exercise and then an apéritif before lunch. Not far from his former hotel he looked up to see his old friend, the photographer, levelling the camera again. He recognized Travers and gave him something like a grin, and it was to Gallois he handed his card. Travers was considerably amused as Gallois read it and then turned back for a word or two.

What the two talked about Travers did not know, for he had walked politely on. Gallois caught him up with an expression of delight on his face. Travers took it for amusement.

"An enterprising fellow that," he said, "Quite cosmopolitan in his catering for all nationalities."

"Why not?" Gallois said. "Look at the cars in the parks there, and you will find the places of all the countries in Europe. But this idea of a photograph pleases me. You will not object if I obtain one? An enlargement, perhaps, which makes an excellent souvenir to exhibit in my room."

"That's a good idea," Travers told him. "I wouldn't mind having one myself. That country-man of yours deserves to be patronized."

"But he is not French."

"Not French?"

Gallois shrugged his shoulders. "For once you have not observed, or perhaps you have not heard him speak. I am of the opinion that he is American or even English."

So flabbergasted was Travers that he was blinking away in the sun as he polished his glasses. Then he tried a revenge with a gentle pull on the leg of Gallois.

"There is something else he may be."

"And what is that?"

Travers whispered mysteriously. *"Perhaps he is Bariche!"*

After lunch, with the weather so tremendously hot, Gallois had a siesta of an hour, and then Travers proposed that he should get out the car for a tour of the countryside. He had prepared a route with which Gallois was wholly in agreement—along the road half-way to Cannes, up to St. Isare, on to Gevrol-les-Vignes and home by Lizou. Everything went according to schedule, and before half the trip was over Gallois had more than once congratulated Travers on the excellence of his choice. From the mountains they more than once stopped and looked back. The views were superb, but it was not only the turquoise sea, veined by the currents with opalescent greens; there were also the shifting colours of the hills, the entrancing vistas of their valleys and gorges, and, far ahead, the grandeur of the Alps. Never, Gallois said, had he so enjoyed a trip. It was he who made the suggestion as they were near Lizou, and he caught sight of the tiny square and its café under the planes.

"Why not take an apéritif here, in the evening cool?"

So they found a table in the shade with the tiny plane-surrounded *place* before them, and Gallois was soon growing poetical.

Lizou, he said, was the ideal haven for one of the artistic temperament. Amid its peace and profound quiet, thought would not be cramped, but it would enlarge and expand itself. In towns one became a member of some herd. Thoughts were disseminated and identity became lost.

Travers was sitting there, eyes on nothing in particular, and with an expression of what seemed interest on his face, so that Gallois was thinking he was finding a sympathy for his theories. But Travers was thinking of something quite different. Quite near them on the main road, a car had just passed and in it was the young man he had seen that previous afternoon at the fork which they would soon be passing, and with his usual curiosity and interest in his fellow men, he was wondering who the young man was and the business that brought him from Carliens to Lizou—or maybe beyond—in the late afternoons.

"It is a theory which pleases you?" Gallois was saying. "You find it sympathetic?"

"Er—yes," said Travers, suddenly aware that he had not been listening. "But it is getting late. You will permit me to pay the bill?"

"But no, it is I who pay," Gallois said, and at once was getting to his feet and clicking his long fingers as a call to the waiter.

Then as the tiny bill was paid he had a last look round.

"You are fortunate to live in a spot as quiet and peaceful as this," he told the waiter.

The waiter shrugged his shoulders. To-morrow, he said, it would not he so quiet.

"What happens to-morrow?" demanded Gallois.

The waiter said there was the annual cattle fair. Cattle, sheep, and even goats came down from the mountains at the end of the winter, and it was at Lizou that there was held a sale which was famous throughout the district.

"So you see, Lizou has its distractions even for a philosopher," Travers said amusedly as the car moved off once more.

Two miles out of the tiny town they overtook an ancient *autobus*, and crawled behind it till there was room to pass. Travers tried pulling the leg of Gallois again.

"Lizou may be a haven of peace to you," he said, "but it seems to pay somebody to run an *autobus* service for its inhabitants to get out of it."

"Those are what you call in English, the trippers," Gallois said contemptuously. "For my part, if the time comes when I wish to retire, I may even consider this Lizou."

It was after seven o'clock when they were back in the hotel. Velot was doubtless supervising the dinner, but Madame was at the desk.

"You have not been to the circus?" asked Gallois.

"But yes," she said. "It is over an hour since I got back."

"And you enjoyed it?"

She smiled. "It was even better than every one said. Everything was marvellous." Then a cloud came over her face. "Unfortunately I did not see the celebrated Auguste."

"He did not perform?"

Her hand spread in a gesture of resignation.

"He is dead! There was an announcement made, and even the gentleman who made it was overcome by emotion. For myself, it was with difficulty that I did not cry, he spoke so sympathetically."

As they moved off, Gallois seemed perfectly indifferent to the fate of Auguste, but all the evening, whenever he thought of that little white rat, Travers, in spite of himself, felt something very much like gloom.

Wednesday morning dawned, and a sudden restlessness in Gallois betokened the arrival of what might be, for himself, as vital a day as he had ever known. Though nothing whatever had been discovered of the supposed priest he was far from despairing of his arrival at the Toulon rendezvous. As he told Travers, it was in the priest's own interest to keep his identity a secret, which might explain why it was that Toulon had found no trace of him. "When he comes"—Travers nearly said "if"—"what are you going to tell him about the reward? What he asks is really very little, surely? In English money, about three hundred pounds. That isn't a lot, is it, for the apprehension of any one as important as Bariche?"

On the face of Gallois was that dreaminess which always announced that everything had been foreseen and there was a prospect in view.

"To you the sum may seem little," he said, "but he will have to take less. In France we are not so lavish with our money."

"But if he demands it?"

Gallois shrugged his shoulders. "The reward is nothing. The main thing is for me to contact myself with him. Then he will be known and every movement will be observed, until he again makes contact with Bariche. After that, it is not a question of what reward he demands, but of what we shall give."

Whatever Travers thought about all that, he made no comment. There were times when Gallois would seem ruthless and even wholly unprincipled, but Travers was far from wishing to condemn. Every one to his own methods and, as Gallois himself had once said, if you wanted scruples and fair play, then let *messieurs les assassins* commence.

The two strolled before lunch and sat for a time on the beach, and then as the clock on the Hôtel de Ville struck twelve, Gallois remembered that a ceremonial farewell ought to be paid to M. Aumade. Five minutes later they were being shown into his room.

"All holidays come to an end," Aumade said as he shook hands. "I, myself, was spending a holiday among my vines when this affair called me here. You return to Paris? And you, M. Travers, go to Marseilles to await the arrival of your wife?"

Before Travers could reply there was a knock at the door. A man was urgently desiring to see someone in authority. He had information about Rionne.

"His name?" demanded Aumade.

"M. Cippe. He has a restaurant at Furolles."

"Admit him at once," Aumade said. "You gentleman would like to hear his information?"

Gallois said he would esteem it as a favour and an honour. In came M. Cippe and with him a stenographer.

Aumade took his official seat at the desk.

"You have information for us?"

"Yes," said Cippe, and looked round nervously at the array of strangers.

"Then give us the information, please," said Aumade, with a smile time was most friendly. "If there is a beginning, perhaps you will be so good as to commence at it."

Cippe perceived something of a joke and was at once at his ease.

On Thursday last, he said, a man entered his restaurant at about four o'clock in the afternoon in company with a lady who wore a veil. The man was the man of the photograph which had been posted outside the Town Hall at Furolles. This man asked if there was a private room where he and the lady could have tea, and he was shown upstairs to the spare dining-room where tea was brought, and cakes from a neighbouring *pâtisserie*. The bill was paid and the couple left. Where they went he had no idea.

"You are positive, M. Cippe, that the man was the Gustave Rionne of the photograph?" asked Aumade.

"Positive. Also he had on his hand the scar which is mentioned. I noticed it myself when he was paying the bill."

"Ah!" said Aumade and nodded. "You are a man of acute perception. Without doubt it was Rionne. And the lady? You can describe her?"

"Alas," said Cippe, "there is little that I remember."

"She did not speak?"

"Not a word."

"She seemed anxious to avoid notice?"

Cippe smiled. "Afterwards that is what I thought myself. It is rare that a lady wears a veil nowadays."

Aumade gave him a nod of praise. "But what was she like? Her clothes, for instance. Her height; the colour of her hair beneath her hat?"

In ten minutes something like a description was slowly put together. She had the manner of a lady. She was well, even smartly dressed, in dark clothes, and there was a white feather or ornament in her dark, or black hat. Her hair was dark and her clothes fitted well. That was all the evidence which Cippe could produce, except that he thought her age would be about thirty or thirty-five. To make still more sure that the man he had seen was really Rionne he was to be taken for a sight of the body.

Aumade seemed delighted. "Now we begin," he said. "It is a pity that you gentlemen are not able to remain to find out whether or not we arrive."

But the farewells had to be concluded and the two departed. It was one o'clock when they came out into a dazzling light.

"Well," said Travers, "we seem to have arrived once more at the old precept—*cherchez la femme.*"

Gallois seemed amused and indifferent. "For my part, I still find it difficult to be interested much in this Rionne. As for the lady, doubtless she has already returned to Switzerland. She becomes the needle in the stack of hay."

"But she may not be the one who killed him," Travers said.

"Why not?" Then he realized. "You mean that to have entered the lavatory of the men would have been too conspicuous?"

"Well, wouldn't it?"

Gallois shrugged his shoulders again. "All that becomes the affair of M. Aumade. A week or two and nothing more will be heard." He chuckled. "M. Aumade will return to his vines and thank God also that he has disembarrassed himself of a rogue."

It was three o'clock when the Rolls moved off towards Toulon. Travers, if only to show an optimism which he was far from feeling, had paid his own bill and put all his luggage in the car and said farewell to Carliens. There was no need for hurry on the journey, for the preliminary business which Gallois had at Toulon would not take long. All that was to be arranged was for men to be ready to follow the priest when he left the rendezvous.

The two parted on the outskirts of the city where Gallois took the precaution of taking a tram. Travers was to see no more of him till the very moment of the meeting with the priest, but his instructions were that just before six o'clock he was to sit at the same seat as Charles, to whom he would give the necessary and surreptitious explanations, and then be a witness to the meeting. When it was over there would be nothing to do but wait.

Travers parked the car, rediscovered an English-owned café, had tea and took a scroll round. His own excitement was increasing as six o'clock drew near. For the life of him he could not help peering at this passer-by and that and wandering if by chance he was rubbing elbows with Bariche. At a quarter to six he was in the Place de la Liberté and looking for Charles. There were two seats on which he might have been, but he was on neither and then it was too late to look longer, for the clock on the hotel opposite was striking the hour. At that very moment Gallois appeared as if from nowhere, and was on the steps of the Syndicat building. At once he was approached by a man.

Travers's heart missed a beat, and then, almost at once, something curious appeared to be happening. The man was not in the garb of a priest. He was a short, rather plump man with a neat black moustache, and he and Gallois were gesticulating away as if at cross-purposes. Then Gallois was raising to heaven hands that looked like the hands of despair. His shoulders drooped resignedly and the two were all at once crossing the road and coming towards the Place. Travers got to his feet, fingers uneasily at his glasses.

CHAPTER VI
THE GOOD FORTUNE OF CHARLES

THREE OTHER MEN were on the same seat as Travers. Gallois gave a glance at them, motioned, and passed on. A few yards ahead, in the direction of the railway station, he halted in a strategic position, with the Syndicat building still beneath his eye. His manner was agitated as he made the introductions.

"Dr. Debran," he said in French, "brings bad news. It is about Charles. He has had a bad accident."

Travers was staring.

"Oh, no," cut in the doctor. "On your return you will find him, I hope, reasonably well. A day or two and he should be quite himself again. It is possible, if my colleague, Dr. Favre, agrees, that he may return here to-morrow."

Again Gallois was raising hands of incomprehension and despair.

"But why should he be at Lizou? Everything is extremely urgent. I must remain here to see a man who ought to have arrived just now." He turned to Travers.

"My friend, will you accompany the doctor to Lizou? His own car was punctured, so he hired a car to bring him here. Return to Lizou, both of you, in your car, and later perhaps I shall be able to come in the car which the doctor hired."

Dr. Debran was perfectly agreeable and thought the arrangement an excellent one. Gallois was given his telephone number and gave in return that of police headquarters.

"Meanwhile," Gallois said, "my profound gratitude, He is not without interest to me, this M. Rabaud. As for your malaria, may I hope it will soon be better."

"It is nothing," Debran said. "Yesterday was different, but to-day it has almost gone. This gentleman and I will return immediately then to Lizou, and later perhaps we shall see you."

Gallois was off at once. Travers repeated his name to Debran in case he had not caught it.

"Travers," he said. "Travers," and made quite a good hand of it, "You speak excellent French, M. Travers."

"Not as good as I should wish," Travers told him. "Perhaps you will speak slowly so that I can be absolutely sure to understand."

Their business took them no more than a minute or two, for the doctor had only to arrange about his hired car, then there was nothing else to do but to find the side street where the Rolls was parked, and at once they were off again. Travers liked the look of the doctor. He was a much younger man than he had seemed at a distance, only about forty perhaps. His manner had been charming enough, but now there was no talk between them till the car had left the tricky traffic of the town, and then, at the doctor's direction, was turning left from the coast road and already beginning to ascend.

"Would you be so good as to tell me all about the accident?" Travers asked.

It was quite a long story. On that Monday night, as had been hinted, the doctor was feeling none too well. A touch of malaria, in fact, was imminent and he took a stiff dose of quinine. He was going to bed early and had actually gone upstairs when Gabrielle, his sister, fetched him, for there was Grandier, the *cantonnier,* with news of the accident. Debran heard what he had to say, put what he thought he would need in the bag, and went off at once. The *cantonnier* had already contrived to lift M. Rabaud from the car, and there he was lying unconscious. The two carried him to the doctor's house where the wound was stitched, and he was put to bed. Gabrielle, who had been a nurse, kept the unconscious man under observation during the night, as the doctor's malaria had become worse.

On the Tuesday morning the patient was still unconscious. Debran was feeling pretty queer himself and thought it necessary to have not only help, but a second opinion, so he rang his colleague, Dr. Favre of Gevrol.

Gabrielle discussed the case with Favre over the 'phone and in the afternoon Favre himself arrived. His opinion was that the patient should recover consciousness at practically any time and was in no serious danger. Debran, in spite of his fever, was present at the interview. Gabrielle snatched some sleep later and again watched the patient at night.

"It is a pity that I was not able to observe him myself," Debran said. "I would like this kept in strict confidence as I have not mentioned it even to M. Favre, but I am of the opinion that the patient may have recovered consciousness in the night and then have fallen into an exhausted sleep, which lasted till this afternoon. Such cases are far from uncommon, but at any rate it was at three o'clock this afternoon that he was really awake and fully conscious. My own fever had practically gone and I saw him at once and told him that I had taken the liberty of going through his pockets and had found nothing to indicate even his name, so I was not able to communicate with his friends. Also, at any hour, as I told you, we expected him to recover consciousness. Naturally I did not want to excite him in any way, but he gave me the name of M. Gallois and told me where I should find him at six o'clock. Naturally I therefore came at once, My own car was punctured, but I hired one from Lizou. My sister, I should have told you, notified M. Favre, so he may be at Lizou at this moment."

"And how was M. Rabaud in himself?" said Travers,

"Just as I told you. Naturally he complains of pains in the head, and there was a certain amount of nausea. Still we gave him a little nourishment—milk and brandy and egg—and then when I came away he was dozing again."

"And you really feel better yourself?"

"Well, not completely," he said. "But the attacks are nothing nowadays. They are less frequent and less serious."

The conversation turned to himself. He had been a military doctor in Morocco and it was there he had caught the malaria, which had ultimately forced him to return to civil life. About a year ago he had settled in Lizou, and later on his sister had decided to keep house for him. At first he had not intended to practise, but to do some research work perhaps as a hobby, but then old Dr. Favre of Gevrol had approached him with the proposition that he should relieve him of some of his patients in the Lizou direction of his extensive, and now too trying, practice. Debran had been only too pleased to agree.

"And yourself, M. Travers," he said, "you are on a holiday?"

Travers told him all about it, and added that M. Gallois the friend he had happened to run across at Carliens, and whom Debran himself had just met, was quite a famous man—no other than Inspector Gallois of the Sûreté.

The doctor looked startled, then was shaking his head. "And I treated him as if he were an ordinary person."

Travers laughed. "Why not? No one, I assure you, is more unassuming than my friend Gallois."

Debran was still shaking his head. "He will have to pardon me. When one has been abroad as long as I have he gets out of touch with things, and M. Rabaud did not mention—"

"Pardon me," said Travers, "but would you mind referring to him as Charles? We always think of him as Charles."

The doctor smiled, "I quite understand that, I think, but this Charles referred to M. Gallois and not Inspector Gallois."

"You really mustn't worry your head about it," Travers told him. "The inspector would be the last man in the world to claim respect. By the way, he is only down here on holiday, At least, there was some conference or other he had to attend at Nimes—he and Charles—and then he took a brief holiday along the coast."

The doctor was excitedly remembering something. "There was a murder in Carliens. We heard all about it in Lizou, and there's a photograph of the man stuck up on one of our plane trees in the square. Did the murder happen while you were there?"

"Yes," Travers said. "It did actually happen while we were there, but it doesn't, of course, have anything to do with Inspector Gallois. He was leaving Carliens for Toulon to-day in any case."

Now that conversation had taken well over an hour and the car was now coming down from the plateau and into Gevrol. Dusk was in the sky and in a few minutes it was dark.

"Would you mind slowing down just here?" Debran said when they were well in the town. "It might be better to make sure whether Dr. Favre has gone to see the patient. If he has not, he might perhaps like to come with us."

Travers drew up before the house which was indicated, and in five minutes Debran came out with his colleague. Favre was quite an old man, though active enough, with the most ferocious of white eyebrows, but he turned out to be quite mild mannered and Travers was finding him rather amusing. His personal appearance, for instance, seemed of no consideration whatever, for his black clothes had an ancient greenish look, his linen was far from clean, and the first thing he did on entering the car was to take a terrific pinch of snuff from a tin box which he then passed ceremoniously to his colleague and Travers, But when he and Debran began discussing the patient, Travers found their technicalities beyond him, especially as the doctor was sitting behind and was bellowing to make himself heard.

The journey was a slow one, with the winding and unfamiliar road, and twice they had to pull up while belated flocks of sheep went by them. Then at the scene of the accident Debran suggested that Travers should slow up, and the lights of the car revealed the scene. The local gendarme had reconstructed everything from the brake-marks of the car and a new breakage in the ruined wall, it was plain that the car had been hit by another one and the police had the matter in hand, but the car itself had been taken away to the local garage and put to rights, and was, the doctor believed, ready at that moment to drive away.

Travers moved on slowly round the bend, and there was the doctor's house, looking like a tiny English vicarage set among its trees, with the hills almost overhanging it. There was no actual drive to the front door, but a side lane which led to the garage behind the house. Just beyond the lane Debran suggested the car should stop, and the three got out. Almost at once there was a flashing on of a light, and, standing in the porch as if to welcome them, was a woman.

From the twenty yards distance Travers could see she was wearing a black dress with what looked to him like a broad white trimming at the neck, and the effect was so much that of a uniform that he knew she must be Gabrielle, the sister of Debran. As he came nearer he saw it was no uniform but a quiet, charming frock. And she was much younger than he had thought. Thirty-five or younger, he guessed, and it was not till much later that he knew she was actually forty,

"*Eh bien, Gabrielle. Tout va bien?*" Debran was calling.

"*Trés trés bien,*" she said with a slow assurance.

A charming voice, Travers thought, and, now he was seeing her closely, a charming woman. The face was not handsome but full of character, and there was a poise and an air of quiet confidence about her. Her brown hair was lovely and her eyes gentle and expressive.

"He is asleep?" old Favre asked in that thin voice of his.

"He had a short nap and now he is awake again," she said, "There was really no need to come when I rang you up." She was turning to Travers with a grave smile. *"C'est M. Gallois?"*

Debran broke in at once with explanations, and Travers was grateful that his French was so careful and precise.

"If I may be pardoned," Travers said, "I would like to warn you that M. Rabaud will be very astonished to find me here instead of M, Gallois. He has no idea that I am even in France. He will be pleased to see me, but—"

"You think it will be a shock," Debran said, and nodded thoughtfully as he turned to Favre. "We will have a look at him."

But there were steps outside and a young man in dungarees appeared at the open door.

"It is Louis, come to mend the puncture," Gabrielle said, and went off to give instructions. She caught up with Travers on the landing. He had been snuffing the air and was recalling the smells of an English country surgery.

"Perhaps you will wait here," she said, opening a door. "In a minute perhaps they will be ready."

"Thank you," Travers said, and gave a nervous clearing of the throat, "M. Rabaud, if you will permit me to say so, has been very fortunate in his nurse."

She looked surprised for a moment, then smiled. "It is my brother that you should thank, and M, Favre. I have done nothing."

Travers shook his head. "We are grateful to all of you. If my French were better I would express myself better."

She smiled again and was gone. A door was opening across the landing and he heard her speak, and then there was Charles's voice and the thin, squeaky accents of old Favre.

Another minute and he was being called in. Charles was propped up on the pillows against which his face seemed less pale than it was, but against that pallor of the face the eyes looked dark and enormous.

Travers smiled affectionately and pressed the hand that Charles slowly raised.

"And how are you, Charles? Better?"

Charles nodded almost with a jauntiness.

"And you know why I happen to be here?"

"It is all explained," Charles said, and though the smile was brave enough, his voice was tired, "M. Gallois is remaining in Toulon in case his friend arrives. If not he will be coming here."

The doctor had been right, Travers was thinking, and then was finding his French suddenly inadequate.

"I am not used to visiting invalids," he told the room, "and I find my French has gone. What I would like to do is to tell him in English how reckless he has been and how thankful I am that he is no worse."

"M. Rabaud speaks English?" Gabrielle asked.

"Not at all badly," Travers told her, "His English is quite as good, perhaps, as my French."

Then she was speaking English herself.

"I speak it a little also," she said with a smile of hesitation. "I do not have the practice."

"But you speak admirably," Travers told her delightedly.

She was actually blushing as she shook her head. Old Favre cut in importantly.

"I think now that he should rest. A little nourishment, perhaps. A sedative. What do you think?"

He and Debran began conferring. Gabrielle nodded for Travers to say good night to Charles. Travers patted his hand.

"Sleep well, my friend, and have no anxieties. In a minute or two I will ring up M. Gallois and give him your news. To-morrow morning you will be seeing us both."

He Found Gabrielle in the hall and she looked up the Toulon number for him. Gallois was waiting at the other end of the line. The gentlemen had not turned up, he said, guardedly, so he had had dinner and was coming at once, even if Charles was asleep when he arrived.

The two doctors came down and Gabrielle reported that the puncture was mended.

"And you really think the patient is going on well?" Travers asked.

"Yes," Debran said. "Exceedingly well. He still complains of headache, naturally, but there is less nausea. To-morrow morning you should see a great difference."

"In my opinion there is no necessity for me to come to-morrow," Favre said. "Ring me up in the morning when you feel inclined. If anything should happen—well, you will judge."

Debran explained that he was driving the old doctor home in his car and he would be seeing Travers on his return. When the two had gone Travers was wondering about accommodation for the night and was thinking of ringing up a Carliens hotel, Gabrielle looked surprised.

"But you will stay here to-night," she said. "Both you and M. Gallois. I am already preparing two rooms."

Travers protested, but she insisted. The favour would be hers and her brother's, she said. It was rare that they had a chance of entertaining guests, and, speaking for her brother especially, it was often somewhat lonely in Lizou.

An hour later many things had happened. Travers was installed in the little *salon,* and when Charles had been attended to he was called to the dining-room where a meal was ready. The doctor had returned, and again Travers was protesting. He was assured that it was as easy to prepare for three as it was for two. During the meal the doctor twice went upstairs. He was not hungry in any case, he said. After those boots of malaria, it was always some days before he really regained his normal healthy appetite.

Fortunately that night he would be able to sleep for there was little sickness in the district and there were no babies expected, The last news about Charles was that he was sleeping healthily, and it was Travers who suggested that, the doctor should go to bed, and after all might not he and Gallois go to a Carliens hotel for the night and save all the bother? The doctor refused to hear a word. Two rooms had been prepared and Gabrielle would be hurt if they were not used. Just then there was a sound of a car.

* * *

The porch light was switched on and the two went down to meet Gallois.

It was with a considerable warmth that Gallois shook the doctor's hand. The two went upstairs, and by a night-light at the bedside Gallois saw Charles in a peaceful sleep.

"My sister is spending the night in that room there," the doctor said. "She is a very light sleeper and would hear at once if he stirs."

"But I, why should I not watch in the room?" Gallois said.

The doctor's hand went up to pat him on the shoulder. "You require rest like all of us, and in the morning the patient will no longer be a patient. Another day's rest perhaps and he may be able to leave. After that, no excitement for a day or two and plenty of rest and, but for the scar, he will think this accident has never occurred."

Gabrielle had left coffee for them in the *salon* and the doctor produced an excellent cognac. The three chatted for a time, and already Gallois was uttering his thanks for all that the doctors and Gabrielle had done. Debran seemed touched by the warmth of Gallois, but claimed that what he himself had done had been only a very modest duty.

"It was a responsibility, l grant you," he said. "I very nearly rang up the hospital at Carliens in the morning and had him removed there. Then I thought perhaps it was dangerous, and in the afternoon Favre dissuaded me. I'm afraid my thoughts were not very clear."

"That cursed malaria," Gallois said, "I know it through a friend of mine who is a sufferer. But your sister must have had her hands full, with you to look after as well as Charles."

The doctor smiled to himself. "Gabrielle is a fine character. Though you would not think it, as brave as a lion. If I had been unable she would not have hesitated to put in the stitches herself."

It was after eleven when the three went up to bed. In spite of the excitement of that day and a strange bed. Travers knew somehow that he would not lie long awake. There was a feeling of comfort and security about the house and its inmates, and a warmth in the thought of their simple, unforced hospitality. Lizou had long since been in bed and everywhere there was a hushed quiet. Through his open window there was no sound but the faint rumble of the mountain stream as it made its way through the narrow gorge, and it was to that soothing background that almost at once he fell asleep.

CHAPTER VII
A NEW SENSATION

Travers was down early, as he thought, but Gabrielle Debran and the doctor had been up for an hour and had already breakfasted.

Overnight he had thought her complexion pale, but now there was colour in her cheeks and he knew it was the tiredness from the spells of watching over Charles that had made her look so tired and drawn in the artificial light, She had had a good night, she said. The patient had stirred only occasionally and each time had gone to sleep practically at once.

"How is he this morning?" Travers asked.

"Much better," she said. "The doctor is with him now. But here he is, and M. Gallois."

The doctor's greeting was most cordial and he was anxious to know if Travers had slept well. After breakfast Charles, he said, would be visible for a few minutes.

"You are really satisfied with him?" Travers wanted to know.

The doctor shrugged his shoulders with an amused indifference.

"Just a slight buzzing in the head, but that will go. Why, the nausea that he complained of has gone already. Now he's actually complaining of hunger!"

He went to the kitchen to discuss with Gabrielle what Charles's meal was to be. Travers and Gallois strolled as far as the road.

"You're looking worried," Travers said. "It isn't about Charles?"

Gallois shook his head. "It is not Charles who worries me; he has the lives of a cat. It is last night that worries me and why this informer did not arrive." He shook his head again. "But I am not worried. That is not the word. It is because there is something which does not make good sense."

He was halting and taking Travers's arm as if to force him to listen.

"Think, if you will, one minute. When he speaks on the 'phone his voice to me is genuine and I, Gallois, do not make mistakes. I tell myself it is not a trick that someone makes to bring me to Toulon. And there was the talk of a reward. I ask myself again if that is some trick to obtain money, and then I know it is not. This informer knows that we do not part with money until we have satisfied ourselves." His shoulders raised with something of exasperation. "And there are other things which I know, which even to you I cannot explain. I tell you that here, in my heart, I know that Bariche is alive, and that this informer knows also that Bariche is alive."

"There is something I've been thinking," Travers said. "Last night he expected to see you absolutely alone. Suppose he was a minute or two late, wouldn't he have been frightened away at seeing you with Debran? Surely it would have looked to him as if you were trying to lure him into some trap."

The shoulders of Gallois raised again, and his palms spread to something of a helpless cringe.

"That also I think of, and I do not know. But at six o'clock I shall he in Toulon again at the rendezvous. If this informer does not appear I will return to Paris. Some day perhaps he will ring me again. Until then this cursed Bariche remains dead."

Gabrielle was calling them. Their breakfast was ready, and as the early morning was so delightful she had placed the table beneath the awning over the *salon* window, and the two ate their *croissants* and drank their coffee out in the lovely morning cool. There was a little pot of marmalade which Travers rather thought had been obtained especially for himself as an essential to an English breakfast.

"Isn't it curious," he said to Gallois, "the thousands of wonderful people there are in the world whom one ought to meet but never will? When we were through here the other afternoon we never had the slightest idea there were people here called Debran, and now here we are. Guests, as it were of two of the kindest and nicest people I ever met in my life."

"Yes," said Gallois. "For me, as a Frenchman, there is a pride that you should discover people so generous and of such good heart. It is the Debrans, my friend, and not the politicians and the *blagueurs,* who are the true France."

Travers was not at all disposed to argue the point. That morning he was on such good terms with himself and so romantically minded that he would have agreed with almost anything. Romance—though that perhaps was not quite what he would have called it—was everywhere about him, and not only in the beauty of the morning. There was romance in the scent of the pines and spring flowers; in the near ridge that faced them across the valley, and the red terraced earth with its young vines. There was a romance in the very thought that he was in France at all, and even in the whiff of Gallois's French tobacco.

No sooner had Travers lighted his pipe than the doctor was joining them. Charles was now presentable, be said, and might be seen for a moment. Never had he known a concussion patient so resilient.

"But why the ominous shake of the head?" he asked Gallois. "This is only an experience he has had. I admit he was fortunate, but a few days in bed are an easy price to pay for being alive. Don't you think so?"

"It is not that," Gallois said. "To my mind he had no right to embark on adventures with a car."

"You are not to be angry with him." Gabrielle was in the porch and shaking her head reprovingly at Gallois. "You yourself were young once."

Gallois shrugged his shoulders. "But I did not take strange cars among mountains."

She laughed. "Perhaps because there were no cars and no mountains. But I am not going to have him scolded. In a sense he is my patient and I like him."

"Better than myself?" asked Gallois with an unexpected raillery.

"Much better," she told him promptly. "Better even than M. Travers."

The doctor laughed as he got to his feet. It was high time for a few minutes with Charles, he said, and doubtless the bark of M. Gallois was infinitely worse than his bite.

But there was something of reproach in the sad smile upon the face of Gallois as he halted just inside the bedroom door, and with a quiet melancholy surveyed the occupant of the bed.

"*Eh bien?*" was all he said.

Charles shrugged his shoulders, caught for a moment the winking eye of Travers and then grinned feebly. Travers felt an enormous desire to laugh. There was a charm of comedy and something superbly French about it all, with the snub nose of Charles giving a roguishness and somehow dominating the scene as completely as if it had been the nose of Cyrano. Gallois approached the bed, patted a hand, then drew up a chair for himself. Travers took the end of the bed.

"And you are feeling yourself again?" Gallois asked.

"Almost," Charles told him. "My head still buzzes a little, but the doctor's certain it will be gone in a day or two."

Gallois leaned over and examined the stitches, and his head was shaking reprovingly. "All your life that scar will remind you—" He broke off in time. "But the car in which you were driving. It belongs to some friend?"

Charles told him the whole story. Gallois took down the address of the Toulon garage. He would ring them at once, he said, and reassure them, and, as the doctor was positive the car was already repaired, he would drive is to Toulon himself that morning.

"The priest did not arrive then?" Charles said with something of diplomacy and certainly relief.

"Never mind the priest," Gallois told him dryly. "Let us confine ourselves to this accident of yours. Tell us how it happened."

Charles told him what he could. All he remembered was the lights of the lorry, and a tremendous lorry it must have been. There was the overturning of the car and then a tremendous crack on the skull, and, as to that last, what must have happened was that he had been thrown across the car and had then crashed back against the comparatively sharp upright of the door.

After that he had had the most fantastic dreams which now seemed to be causing him a certain ironic amusement. All the time he had been drowning in the depth of the sea and trying to get to the surface, and then suddenly it was as if something ceased to press on his brain, and there he was in bed. The sun was shining and the first thing he heard was a distant clock striking three and he was wondering in a sort of childish, bewildered way what three o'clock it was and where he was and if he was alive at all. Then Gabrielle came in and at once she was calling excitedly to someone, and it turned out to be the doctor, who appeared in a dressing-gown and as if not properly awake.

"He was still recovering from his malaria and had been asleep," put in Travers, always ready with an explanation.

Charles said the doctor himself had explained and apologized for that, but Charles had been more anxious about the car than himself, but when he referred to the accident of "last night" the doctor smiled and Charles learned that he had been unconscious for thirty-six hours or more. So queer did it seem to lose a whole day of his life, and so incredulous must he have looked, that the doctor told Gabrielle to bring him the newspaper to convince him.

"That is nothing," Gallois said. "Rest for a moment now while I tell you something. In the Great War when I was operated on for shrapnel, I knew the doctor who was about to perform the operation, and just at the very moment of receiving the anaesthetic I was asking about his brother, but I did not catch his reply, so I repeated the question. Then I repeated it again and then I found was asking the question of myself, for I was back in my bed and the operation was already over. Two hours had gone by since I put that first question but, as far as I was concerned, there had been an interval of two seconds. But to continue your own experiences. What did you feel like in yourself when you woke?"

What Charles now recalled most was the pain in the head and the nausea, and how he seemed to hear things none too distinctly. But he did hear Gabrielle and her brother talking about a Dr. Favre who had seen him on the previous day. Then Dr. Debran asked his name. Had he any friends who should be advised of what had happened? Then it turned out that the bag which had been in the car had been stolen as well as all the money from his pockets, and even his wrist-watch. The doctor had said he was not to worry about anything. The police would soon recover the missing things and he himself would go to Toulon and bring back M. Gallois. All he was to do was to rest and then, almost at once, he was given what he guessed was brandy and milk. Either the doctor or Gabrielle came in every few minutes and then the doctor examined him again and gave him a tonic. If he felt like sleeping he was to do so. He heard the distant clock strike four, and then he had slept for an hour or two and felt very much better when he woke. Gabrielle tidied him up, and almost at once M. Travers arrived.

"You owe a debt of enormous gratitude," Gallois was beginning, and then Gabrielle came smilingly in. There was a lot of talking, she said, and now the patient must rest. Gallois rose at once with an amusing docility.

"In the morning we shall see you again," he told Charles. "Meanwhile, you're to obey implicitly every instruction of those who know better than yourself."

He shook Charles's hand and went mournfully out. Travers gave a friendly grip and followed him. Almost at once Gabrielle was coming down the stairs.

"What did you mean about not seeing him till the morning?" she asked Gallois. "This afternoon perhaps you might be able to spend as much as an hour upstairs."

"But he is in no danger."

"Of course he is in no danger," she said and hesitated for a moment. "But we hoped that both of you would stay."

Gallois shrugged his shoulders in preliminary protest. Then she was anticipating all he had to say.

"It would do you good," she said, "to have the pure air of the country for another day. There are magnificent walks here among the mountains. If my brother had been quite well he would have gone with you, but I can show you the paths, and if you and M. Travers prefer not to return for lunch, you can lunch at Gevrol."

Gallois began explaining, and then the doctor came in. He added his own invitation, but Gallois with an enormous regret and an enormous gratitude still insisted that he must go. His business in Toulon was official and important and there was the matter of Charles's car. Travers regretted too, but he would have to accompany Gallois, though in the morning they would both return and that same evening they would be sure to ring up.

The doctor and his sister looked so genuinely disappointed that Travers had an idea.

"It's not absolutely necessary for me to be at Toulon till the evening," he said to Gabrielle. "Would you permit me to drive you somewhere for a brief holiday? There are friends perhaps you would like to see somewhere, and you could show me the countryside."

But now Gabrielle had to refuse. There was the house to look after, and her brother, and that afternoon she had thought of making up for lost sleep.

"But you need not worry about me," the doctor said.

"Exactly," cut in Travers, and had a new idea. "Did you see the circus which was at Carliens?"

She looked astonished, as well she might, at the unexpected question.

"It was really marvellous and worth any one seeing," Travers was going on. "It's at Cannes this afternoon, so why shouldn't I drive you there. Then we can come back here and I can see Charles and then go on to Toulon, and everything will fit in perfectly splendidly."

She was shaking her head. "I am foolish perhaps, but I always dislike circuses. It's the animals, and how they have to perform."

"But you can shut your eyes when we come to the animals," Travers said, and the smile was suddenly turning to one of reminiscence. "There was one animal you would have loved—a little white rat called Auguste. He was perfectly delightful and brave as a lion—if lions fly through the air."

"You're talking in riddles," she told him, and smiled. "But I don't think I will go all the same." And then in English, "You are very kind."

Gallois emitted something of a chuckle. "Another week in the company of M. Travers," he said in English, "and you would be speaking an English better than my own. But if you will excuse us, we must return at once to Toulon."

When he had uttered his thanks for the hospitality which he and Travers had already received, he insisted that such hospitality must not also include Charles. In the morning the doctor's bill must be ready, including that of Dr. Favre. There would also be some reward for the *cantonnier*.

There would be plenty of time to think of all that, the doctor told him and, now he remembered it, some time that day, if he felt equal to it, Charles would have to sign an official statement for the local police, both about the accident and the property that had been stolen.

The two started off for the local garage in Travers's car. Just round the bend Gallois asked if Travers would wait for a minute. There was something he wished to ask which, though to Travers it might sound fantastic, he himself preferred to accept as instinct. It was a feeling of being involved in something strange. It was something like a burning of the ears, for instance, when you wondered if people were really talking about you. It was the alarming feeling as of things happening which could neither be seen nor heard. Perhaps it was a reaction after the anticipation of the interview with the informer and the arrival in its place of that extraordinary accident to Charles, and there Gallois came to his question. *Was it an accident?*

Travers stared. "You mean, someone tried to kill him?"

"Well, yes."

"But surely Charles has not an enemy in the world?"

"But might he not have been mistaken for myself?"

Travers stared again.

"But how on earth could he be? How could any one possibly know he was coming here? He didn't make up his mind to go anywhere till the Monday afternoon, and he wouldn't have come here at all if he hadn't lost his way."

Gallois shook an obstinate head. The more inexplicable a thing was, the greater the need for patience in seeking an explanation. The newspapers, as he pointed out, had all announced that conference at Nîmes, which was an annual event and not without importance. Later the newspapers published a list of all the delegates, and the name of Charles had been bracketed with that of Gallois as if the two of them were one. Gallois himself had left unexpectedly early, so why should someone not have mistaken Charles for him and have followed him and arranged the accident, which instead of putting him out of action for a couple of days, should really have killed him outright.

"But my dear fellow," protested Travers. "If a car was following behind Charles's car, how could it have been in touch with the *camion*?—even supposing the *camion* was waiting here at Lizou, which in itself is incredible. How could it have been told just when and how to stage a head-on collision?"

"It is admitted there are difficulties," Gallois said. "Nevertheless there remains also the instinct which assures me that I am not without reason. This car, for instance, that follows the car of Charles. When it sees that Charles takes the road to Lizou, it proceeds to Gevrol and telephones perhaps to the *camion* which is here at Lizou." He shrugged his shoulders. "Then there is the theft. One cannot deny that someone examined Charles when he was unconscious, and took his bag and searched his pockets."

"Yes," Travers said, "but the same person doing all that searching would have known that Charles was not dead. If he wanted to kill him why didn't he kill him then?"

"He thought perhaps he was dead, or about to die."

"If Charles had died, all the papers of the South would have announced the accident. I hate to put in so many objections, but this murderer of yours must be aware by now that Charles is alive. By the way, who is this murderer? Bariche, or someone connected with him?"

"Ah!" said Gallois. "At last we arrive. As it is not impossible that Bariche knew of the intention of the informer and arranged that he should not appear at the rendezvous last night, would it not be in the interest of this Bariche to kill myself, or even Charles?"

Travers shook his head. "If we bring your arguments to a logical conclusion, you and I oughtn't to be going away from Lizou. We ought to be staying behind to keep an eye on Charles. As for the theft of Charles's belongings, the lights of the car were still burning after the accident. I think someone went down to investigate and decided to help himself, and if it comes to that we do not know the *cantonnier*. He might have taken the bag and the money."

Gallois spread his hands resignedly, and the car moved on. The garage people had made a good job of the repairs. The brakes and everything were in perfect order, Gallois was told, but nevertheless he decided that he would not trust himself among the mountains, but take the coast road. There was no necessity, there appeared, to go into Carliens, as the road branched to Furolles.

Travers was proposing to do nothing in particular except to arrive at the Toulon rendezvous at six o'clock. Then Gallois remembered the photographs which ought to be waiting for him at Carliens.

Travers said he would fetch them, and when he had watched Gallois depart, supervised a rapid overhaul of his own car. It was about half-past eleven when he arrived at Carliens. He parked the car and bought some cigarettes, and sat for a few minutes on a bench facing the sea with the Hôtel de Ville at his back.

What he was thinking about was the accident that had happened to Charles. Though he himself was ready enough to attach importance to hunches and instincts, he could not for the life of him find in the theories and apprehensions of Gallois the least foundation of sober fact. For all that he spent a good ten minutes in trying to puzzle out how that lorry could have made a deliberate attack, as it were, upon Charles. Then at last he was giving it up and turning to the French newspaper which he had bought as a kind of afterthought with the cigarettes. One look at it and he was gaping.

AFFAIRE SINISTRE À CARLIENS
DRAME MYSTERIEUX À VILLA SABLONS
L'ASSASSIN DE RIONNE FAIT ENCORE UN COUP MORTEL?

Travers's glasses were off and he was blinking. The murder of Rionne had apparently not been the simple thing for which Gallois had taken it. Whoever had killed Rionne had apparently struck again, and in his excitement Travers was getting to his feet and hooking on his glasses. Then, as his eyes shifted from the beach, he was vaguely aware that someone he knew was crossing the road from the Hôtel de Ville, portfolio beneath his arm. It was M. Aumade, the examining magistrate, and at that same moment, and with a look of surprise, he was recognizing the lean lamp-post figure of Ludovic Travers.

CHAPTER VIII
IS IT BARICHE?

IF AN HOUR previously Travers had been told that he would lunch with M. Aumade at his hotel, he would have regarded the prophecy as an excellent joke. What Travers did not know was that Gallois had given the examining magistrate so flattering an opinion of himself. Praise from the great Gallois was even more than praise, and Aumade had hailed the sight of Travers as a beneficent miracle. The inducement to lunch was to be followed by an invitation to run at least an eye over the case, and through Travers he hoped to excite the interest of Gallois.

Travers's first question was if there was really any connection between the two murders. Aumade ought to have said no, and that the headline in Travers's newspaper was merely the sensationalism of the Press. What he did was to assume an air of mystery. At the moment one could not tell. That a place, hitherto so free from serious crime as Carliens, should now have two murders, was in itself a matter for thought. But throughout the meal he was giving an outline of what had happened and reinforcing it with copies of evidence from his portfolio. What Travers heard was somewhat disjointed, but it is given here in something of logical order.

First, as to Carliens and its villas. These studded the lower slopes of the hills to the north of the town, and one arrived at them by roads which were not of the best, though good enough for light traffic. They were picturesque enough, too, and bore names that were picturesque, such as the Street of the Pines, the Old Terrace and the Lane of the Waterfall. The villas themselves were of all sorts: some quite tiny affairs and others handsome buildings with land and vines. The Villa Sablons was in the Rue des Pins, as select a spot as any, and was the property of a Lyonnais who let it furnished through an agent in Carliens. It was of a handy size for a family of no more than four, with a small front garden requiring practically no upkeep. On its right was a lovely grove of olive trees; on the other side were *pins ombrelles* and some handsome eucalyptuses, the latter overhanging the garden of the neighbouring villa, occupied by a Colonel Brassier.

In March there arrived at Carliens a M. Georges Letoque, and he put up at the Hôtel de la Mer. He was a Swiss and well provided with money, for he opened an account at the bank for close on one thousand pounds, and later increased it by cash deposits to over three thousand pounds. Almost at once he hired the Villa Sablons for three months and installed himself there. A widow—Marie-Louise Dubois—was housekeeper-cook, but did not sleep in, and one day a week a jobbing gardener pottered about outside.

M. Letoque, according to his passport, was born in Annecy of Swiss parents and was forty-two years old. His French was impeccable, and during the Great War he bad fought for France and received that wound in the leg from which he still limped. That last information came from Colonel Brassier with whom Letoque had at once become friendly. He was a fine-looking man with a dark beard and very expressive eyes, and his manners, by all accounts, were as charming as himself. Most of his life had been spent in Brazil, but he had returned to Switzerland on leave and now was taking a three-months' holiday before his return to South America.

His habits seemed to have been fairly simple and he might have been described as a man of the world who could also appreciate quiet. He could frequent the Casino and he could spend hours sitting on the beach. In the evenings he delighted to take his friends out to dinner, and in the day he would often hire a car and take solitary excursions into the countryside, of which he expressed himself as very fond. The Brassiers had introduced him to their friends, and at once he appeared to have become deservedly popular. Who should want to kill such a man seemed inexplicable. And as Aumade pointed out, the sole connection with the killing of Rionne was the fact that both had come from Switzerland to Carliens.

Now to the tragedy itself. On the Tuesday morning, at eleven o'clock—the morning it will be remembered after the stabbing of Rionne—Mme Dubois was tidying up the bedroom at the Villa Sablons when she saw a man in the olive grove. There was nothing necessarily unusual about that because the grove was the property of some unknown from Cannes. What was unusual was the attitude of the man himself, who seemed to be entrenched behind the huge trunk of an ancient olive and keeping the house under observation. Mme Dubois was a person of a suspicious spying nature and instead of reporting to M. Letoque who was reading his paper on the veranda, she peered out herself. The man became aware of her and disappeared. He was a youngish man, dressed in grey, which was all the information she could give, for the olive tree was at least fifty metres off and her eyes were none too good. It was further indicative of her secretive nature that she did not mention the matter to her employer.

So to the Wednesday morning. It was the custom of Mme Dubois to arrive at the villa at nine o'clock, for M. Letoque was a late riser and did not have his coffee till after she arrived. Near the villa she met a man who saluted her extremely courteously and said that the Grand Cirque Pertini was giving a few free seats for their final matinée of that afternoon. She was only too delighted to accept one, and then, before she could ask leave of absence of her employer, he astonished her by saying that he would not be wanting her that afternoon, though she should return at six o'clock to prepare dinner. As that fitted her plans to admiration she saw no reason to mention the circus.

At six o'clock she returned and found M. Letoque lying dead on the floor of the *salon*. He had been shot twice—through the chest at close quarters and through the head at such point-blank range that the revolver must actually have touched him. Nothing had been stolen and nothing disturbed. Medical evidence showed that death had occurred at about half-past three, and at that time Mme Brassier—the Colonel and his daughter were bathing—heard at an interval of a few seconds two sounds, which might have been shots. She took them for backfires, common enough in cars descending the hilly roads.

"And that roughly is all we know," Aumade said. "You have heard nothing which has given you any ideas?"

But M. Aumade was wholly unaware of Travers's fertility as a theorist, and a question was coming at once.

"Could the two men by any chance have been one and the same?"

"Ah!" The gasp was one of admiration. "It was an idea which occurred to me also, and this morning I questioned Mme Dubois again. But first she was taken to the olive grove. The tree was found to be seventy metres away, and her sight, as she said, was none too distinct. But she maintained that the man she saw and the man who gave her the ticket were not the same." He shrugged his shoulders amusedly. "And why, do you think? Because the second man wore sunglasses and had a dark moustache, whereas she was positive—sight or no sight—that the man in the olive grove was clean-shaven and had no glasses, and their clothes, she said, were different. Nevertheless they were the same height and build, though the second man, she thought, was older than the first."

"The glasses and the false moustache alone would account for that," Travers said.

"Exactly. Still, as a witness she did her best. Otherwise I regard her as a person of most unsatisfactory character who had no scruples about spying on her employer or doing anything that would further her own interests. When you see her, I think you will agree."

"The offer of the tickets was genuine?" Travers asked.

"That is what is being discovered at this very moment," Aumade told him. "Fournal is at Cannes making inquiries at the circus." He glanced at his watch. "It is possible that there is already news from him at my office."

When the two arrived back at the Hôtel de Ville news was just being received from Fournal, and in a minute or two Aumade had the telephoned statement in his hand. That story about the circus management giving free tickets was utterly false. Since they conducted their own publicity they gave away practically no free passes at all, and such as they did give were always scrupulously checked. Nevertheless Fournal had personally seen everybody concerned, and all had alibis, even the bill-posters. There had been three passes that could have been used at the Wednesday matinée and all were accounted for. Therefore Mme Dubois had been given a perfectly ordinary ticket which could have been purchased in advance at the circus box-office or from one of the two agencies in Carliens. The opinion of Fournal was—and Aumade was inclined to agree—that it would be absolutely impossible to check up the purchaser. Not only had the man been so vaguely described by Mme Dubois, but there was nothing to prove that he had bought the ticket himself.

M. Aumade's car was waiting, and in five minutes Travers had his first sight of the Villa Sablons. He stood behind the olive tree and recognized it as an admirable vantage-point from which to keep the villa under observation. He saw the veranda and the very chair in which Letoque had been sitting, and then he was seeing the room in which he had been found. There were the marks giving the outline of the body, and from his portfolio Aumade produced photographs, though they were scarcely necessary, for nothing whatever had been disturbed, and it required no great imagination to visualize the scene.

To the right, as one entered the room, was an easy-chair, of typical English fashion. It was the only one in the room and was habitually used by Letoque. Across the room and facing it was one of those gilt spindly arm-chairs, and about it Aumade had something interesting to say.

"This morning, in our reconstruction of the crime, we made the discover from marks revealed on the carpet, and which, if you take this glass I think you will still see, that the chair had been overturned and was then replaced where it is now. Bearing in mind that there were two shots, and taking into account their effects, what is your own opinion of what happened?"

Travers slowly polished his glasses and frowned away in thought.

"Well, Mme Dubois had been disposed of, and Letoque himself admitted the caller, whom he expected, shall we say. Possibly it was the very man who had given Mme Dubois the free ticker, but at any rate he placed that gilt chair and took his own usual seat opposite. What was actually said or what actually happened till the two shots there is no evidence to prove, but the moment came when Letoque leapt from his chair to make an attack, and was shot through the chest as he made it. The assassin had got to his feet and drawn back in alarm, and so overturned the chair. The impetus of his rush carried Letoque here to where he fell. Then the assassin saw he was still living and was taking no chances. He put the muzzle of his gun to his head and blew out his brains.”

Aumade had been nodding in agreement, and for a moment nothing else was said. Travers had winced at the cold horror of that last imagined scene. *Sinistre* was indeed the word.

Whoever it was that fired that second shot, he said to Aumade, must either have hated Letoque as no one ever hated before, or he was executing some pretty terrible revenge. But which way did the murderer leave the house?

Aumade took him through to the back, where rough steps mounted between screening clumps of roses to a stony path that led up through the pines to the road.

“No gun was found?” Travers asked as they came back to the *salon*.

“No gun,” repeated Aumade, “and no finger-prints that are unaccounted for.”

Then all at once he was giving a rather peculiar look.

“You think the assassin is a man. You have some reason for thinking it must have been a man?”

“Not necessarily,” Travers said. “One can scarcely imagine, however, a woman firing that second shot, even if it might have been the natural tidiness of a woman that put back in place the overturned chair.”

Aumade nodded an agreement. “But does not the evidence seem to suggest that the assassin was some person known to Letoque?”

“You mean, that was why he got rid of Mme Dubois who would have recognized the caller?”

“Yes,” said Aumade. “I confess that was in my mind.”

“I was wondering,” Travers said, “if one could tell from his clothes whether he had dressed to receive a man or a woman.”

“That also occurred to us,” Aumade told him, “and all we could say was that the clothes he was wearing were as good as any he possessed.”

“He knew many local women?”

Aumade shrugged his shoulders. “As I told you, Mme Brassier and her stepdaughter introduced him to their friends. Perhaps I am unjust to call him a philanderer, but I have already admitted he was popular." And then dryly: "More perhaps with women than men. With regard to one particular lady—Mme Brassier in fact—there may be developments."

Travers, rather at a loss, could only raise his eyebrows and give a nod as enigmatic as Aumade's own.

When Travers first clapped eyes on the dead Letoque he saw only the head, for the rest of the body was covered. The wound had been washed and cleaned, but Travers took only a hurried glance at the grizzly photographs that had been taken before the extraction of the bullet. One thing his eyes could not avoid—the contortion of agony still in the features of the dead man. But when the head was turned and he saw the unwounded side, he was suddenly frowning. Somewhere or other he had actually seen the dead man, but where he could not for the life of him remember. Then he was shaking his head. He had met him perhaps in the streets in Carliens, and the face in some peculiar way had impressed itself on his mind.

Travers saw the clothes and gave a sniff at the faint odour of scent.

"He was something of a dandy," Aumade said. "His hair and beard were pomaded too."

"But did you not say that he was lame? It was a limp, I believe?"

He raised the sheet to show the scar, which was more of a white discoloration, just below the knee-cap.

Travers looked down at the face again, still slightly puzzled by where he had seen the man, then he went closer.

"Aren't the eyes a strange colour for that colour of hair? You'd have expected brown eyes."

"Ah!" said Aumade. "A thousand pardons. I forgot to tell you what apparently you have already observed for yourself. The head and beard are dyed."

Travers took a glass and examined the scalp.

"I wonder," he said, "if there is any possible means of removing this dye, so that we can obtain a photograph as he normally was." Then he was shaking his head. "But I am afraid not. It is sure to be an ordinary bismuth solution that he used. All the same, the fact that he dyed the hair at all shows that he had something to conceal. The hair of a man of his age ought not to be turning grey, and it's just as easy to bring back hair to a light shade as to turn it black." He had been moving aside the sheet. "His normal hair is fair, as you see."

"Yes," said Aumade. "After all, one does not need to dye what will not be noticed."

"You are making inquiries about his passport?"

"There should be news about that this afternoon," Aumade said. "For my part, I am rather disposed to think the hair was dyed out of vanity." He gave a chuckle as he opened the door and courteously waved for Travers to go through. "If every dandy was a criminal we should have to build several new gaols."

In the ante-room he was informed that Fournal was back from Cannes. Travers at once began taking his leave. If M. Gallois was returning to Paris, he himself would like to return to Carliens, and observe the admirable investigations which were being conducted. No one would be more welcome, Aumade told him, and M. Gallois too if he would be able to return. Meanwhile it was himself who was grateful.

Now if he had known Travers better Aumade would have been aware that for some minutes here had been something on Travers's mind. It was four o'clock, and the first thing that Travers did was to try and get hold of Gallois on the 'phone. The reply was that he was not expected again till after six o'clock. Travers had been 'phoning from the Hôtel de France and there he had a brief talk with Velot, after which he set out for Toulon. He drove fast and after parking the car outside the Place de la Liberté, he had only just time to take a seat facing the Syndicat building as the clock struck six. Gallois was already there, standing patiently and inconspicuously. A few minutes and he went inside; two or three minutes and he reappeared, and as the dock struck the half-hour he was deciding evidently to give it up. A hundred yards on Travers caught him up. What he was going to do, he said, was to ring the Sûreté and find out if any communication had been received there from the informer.

A quarter of an hour later he was with Travers again and shaking his head despondently. All he could suggest was finding an hotel for the night.

"A drink first, I think," counselled Travers, and indicated a suitable spot across the road.

"This is a day of fatigue," said Gallois, when he was able to stretch his long legs beneath a table. "Never in my life do I feel so tired. And you—how did you pass your day?"

Travers told him and Gallois was at once professionally interested. He had read the papers, he said, but only for what they were worth.

"And so our good friend Aumade is again being kept from his vines," was his comment. "Who is this Letoque, do you think? Another member of the gang who came from Switzerland with Rionne and has been killed for the same reason?"

"There are far more unlikely things," Travers told him us the drinks arrived. There was a long whisky-soda for Gallois and a quick one for himself.

"That was good," Gallois said and see down his glass again. "That clears the brain and fortifies the blood. But I was forgetting—you have brought the photographs?"

"Well, no," said Travers. "I was in rather a hurry and I was also of the opinion that you would like to take a look at that second murder case at Carliens yourself."

Gallois looked astonished. "But I return almost at once to Paris."

"But we have to go to Lizou to-morrow to fetch Charles. Which reminds me. There are presents I must buy for the doctor and his sister."

"There is no hurry," said Gallois. "To-morrow is Good Friday and the shops remain open late tonight. But why should you think there should be an anxiety for me to return to Carliens?"

Travers hooked off his glasses and was giving them a slow deliberate polish.

"There are things which I have not yet told you about this Letoque affair which the papers have not printed. But you have already read his description in the papers and I have already told you that his hair was dyed black."

"Yes," said Gallois almost amusedly.

"His forearms were shaved," Travers said. "That shows he was particularly anxious that it should not be known that his hair was dyed. He was really a blond."

"The Swiss often are," Gallois told him with a shrug of the shoulders. "Perhaps, however, you will permit me to change the theory which I put forward in a moment of too much speed. It is possible that this Letoque was the emissary sent by the gang from Switzerland to discover the whereabouts of Rionne and remove him. He would therefore grow a beard and dye his hair so that he should not be known to Rionne."

Travers was smiling even more diffidently as he hooked the glasses on again.

"Well, I will come to the point. You would not be too incredulous if I mentioned some further resemblances between this Letoque and—Bariche?"

"Bariche!" The eyes of Gallois narrowed.

"Bariche had money which he obtained from his victims," went on Travers. "He would necessarily have cash, and it was cash Letoque deposited in the bank at Carliens."

Gallois was still only mildly interested.

"At Auteuil, Bariche was a blond, and clean-shaven. He killed his last victim at Auteuil, and left the body of a man for himself. To go elsewhere in France would have become very dangerous. Then why not go to Switzerland?"

Gallois shrugged his shoulders as much as to ask why not.

"His build and height tally, and his age. His eyes are grey-blue, and I know no method of disguising the colour of the eyes. Further, Aumade assured me in confidence that Letoque was already having an affair with at least one woman."

Gallois gave an inquiring look.

"If you ask me about the lameness," went on Travers, "I should say that Letoque was either not lame at all, or that lameness had occurred through some accident after Auteuil. The scar on the knee looked nothing important. Letoque himself told his friends it was a war wound."

Gallois was frowning and his lean fingers were slowly caressing his chin.

"Then there is Brazil. Letoque had already announced that he was returning there after his leave. Brazil is a very distant country and not the easiest of places for inquiries. Wasn't it the habit of the victims of Bariche to announce suddenly to their relatives that the husband had had an urgent call abroad, and after that nothing more was heard?"

"Yes," said Gallois. "Perhaps, my friend, we will after all return to Carliens. And you have other reasons?"

Travers smiled. He had been none too sure himself of the effect of his theories upon Gallois, but now there was a confidence and in some curious way a relaxation.

"I would like to interest my grandchildren."

"Your grandchildren?" The palms of Gallois spread incredulously. "But, my friend, you have not yet even children."

"There is still time," Travers told him, "and one day perhaps I may tell my grandchildren about Bariche, when they ask me for a story about Bluebeard. It will be an interesting story and they will possibly say, 'Did you ever see him alive, grandfather?' 'Oh, yes,' I shall say unconcernedly. 'I saw him alive and showed him to the famous French detective Gallois, about whom you have often heard me speak, but we neither of us believed it was Bluebeard.'"

The fingers of Gallois rose as if to clutch the air. "When did you show him to me?"

"That night in the Hôtel de France," said Travers. "You remember I said any one might be Bariche? Even the waiter—or that lame man with the black beard?"

"He was Letoque?"

"Yes," said Travers. "He was Letoque, who I'm also fairly sure is Bariche."

CHAPTER IX
GALLOIS IS UNCONVINCED

IT WAS GOOD FRIDAY, a day always associated in the mind of Travers with dishes of dry, tasteless cod, and he was at Lizou where the farewells were being said.

Old Favre had rung up to present his compliments to everybody, and Gallois had some private talk with Debran. The doctor still urged quiet for the patient. It was far from rare, for instance, for pneumonia to supervene after such shocks, though he was fairly confident now that Charles would run little risk.

Gallois in very strict confidence mentioned the accident. The police, particularly those of the prominence of himself and Charles, always had enemies, he said, and fantastic though it might seem to the doctor, an attack was far from an unlikely thing. The doctor heard him with perfect seriousness. He had seen no suspicious characters about, he said, and as for the *cantonnier,* he could vouch for his implicit honesty. Then just before the actual moment of farewell there was a little ceremony—most unexpected and affecting for the Debrans—when the presents were presented: a picnic set for Gabrielle to use on her trips in the mountains, and a travelling-rug for the doctor for winter use in the car. As for the professional bills, Gallois protested that the amounts were absurd. Favre, for instance, had charged only one hundred and twenty-five francs for his visits of the Tuesday and the Wednesday, and his professional advice.

"I'll send him a box of special snuff from London, as soon as I get back," Travers said.

"And if you are in Paris, any of you, you must come and see me," Gallois said. "It does not matter how busy I am, there will always be time for you."

"And if you should ever travel as far as London," said Travers and looked in his wallet for a card, "my wife and I will be only too delighted to see you or to be of any service."

Charles was feeling an emotion. He actually embraced the doctor and it was with much affection that he kissed the hand of

Gabrielle. Suddenly it occurred to Debran that he had not been told where the party were going.

"If there is no hurry to return to Paris, I should stay for a time where M. Charles could enjoy the air and sun," he said.

"There are many little places between Toulon and Marseilles," Gabrielle said, "which will also be handy for M. Travers when he meets his wife. But wait a minute."

She flew back into the house and returned with an hotel address at Mariette which she knew to be a most delightful little resort quite near Marseilles. Gallois took it with many thanks.

"And you will be sure to write and tell us about the patient?" was Debran's last word when the car was at last ready to move off.

"And about yourselves?" added Gabrielle.

So with much waving of hands and with much of real regret, the last glimpses of Lizou were seen. But as far as Gallois was concerned his sadness lasted only a minute. No sooner in fact had the car left the tiny town than he was himself.

"An expensive affair this holiday of yours, as far as concerns yourself," he said to Charles.

Charles grinned. "At Mariette, I shall be able to economize."

"Unhappily we are not going to Mariette," Gallois told him. "We are going to Carliens and shall deposit you at the Hôtel de France. M. Travers and myself have an appointment for ten-thirty, for which we are already late."

As they walked to the Hôtel de Ville, only one like Travers who knew him so well could have discerned in the manner of Gallois the least trace of excitement or anxiety.

"If this Letoque is Bariche, then he is something private for ourselves," he said. "All that M. Aumade will know is that we have a few days of holiday and wish to offer our services. What he will imagine is that we are seeking, with him, the assassin of this Letoque."

Travers assured him that he would be discretion itself.

Gallois smiled dreamily. "For our friend Aumade, it will be the play of *Hamlet* without the Prince of Denmark. Whatever it is that we discover about Letoque, professional honour demands that we impart it, except that Letoque is Bariche."

Aumade was delighted to see them both, and his first anxiety was whether Gallois was acquainted with the case. Travers reassured him and at once Aumade had some information to give.

"We have had news from Switzerland; the passport is a forgery from beginning to end."

Gallois concealed his gratification beneath a smile of even greater melancholy.

"What was his object then in coming to Carliens?"

"Unhappily we have no idea," Aumade told him. "Neither in Berne not in Paris is there any record of his fingerprints."

Gallois shrugged his shoulders. "He was probably some swindler who was planning a *coup*. Since he was provided with ready money, he may even have had in mind some fraud at your Casino. Within a day or two we should know more."

"You would like to see him?"

"Yes," Gallois said, "it is possible that I may recognize him. In my time I have seen a good many rogues and I have been assured that my memory is a tenacious one."

"We have a quarter of an hour," Aumade said. "The Brassier family are arriving for an interview. They are the neighbours and important witnesses of whom M. Travers has doubtless spoken to you."

But when Gallois examined the dead man he had to confess that he had never seen him before.

"There are relatives?" he said.

"None that we know of. And no letters; no private papers—nothing."

Gallois had been lifting the cold sheet and looking at the scar on the knee.

"And what did your surgeon think of this supposed wound?"

Aumade came bustling round at once.

"It is not a wound?"

"If a bullet entered, or shrapnel, there is no trace of where it emerged. If it remained, there are no signs of an operation."

"The scar did not come within the scope of the surgeon's instructions," Aumade said, "which were primarily to ascertain the precise cause of death. I admit that he observed as a matter of interest that the hair had been dyed. However, I will see that he is informed."

He was courteously ushering them out. Then as they were passing one of the waiting-rooms there was a sound of voices in discussion. The Brassier family were already waiting, and apparently in some disagreement as to the evidence they were about to give. Aumade entered the room with a beam on his face and hand outstretched. Gallois and Travers moved on, while the examining magistrate gave in semi-public the friendly greeting that would be incompatible with his official aloofness.

But back in his room he revealed a duplicity that highly recommended itself to Gallois. The Brassiers, he said, imagined they were coming in together, but he was having them singly.

"I need not ask you to note their reactions to certain questions which, though not fully comprehensible to yourself, have nevertheless been most carefully framed. You will also understand later why it is Mme Brassier who will be coming in last."

Colonel Brassier entered, and to him, as later to the others, Aumade expressed regret for the trouble he was giving him, and thanks in anticipation for a co-operation with the law. He was a wizened, disillusioned-looking man in the late sixties.

The details of his evidence do not matter, but the gist was this. He had been regretting for some time his too hasty friendliness with Letoque. He was almost certainly jealous of him, but on account of his popularity or for some personal reason to do with his wife or daughter was not clear. He had been fulsome in his introduction of Letoque to his circle of friends, and to retract now the flattering recommendations he had given would be to injure his own reputation. And he had one interesting revelation to make. Letoque, he said, claimed to have fought in the Argonne and, when pressed by the Colonel, who was insatiable in the matter of war details, said he had served with the 177th Infantry. But, the Colonel now said, information of his own had been available about the campaign in the Argonne, and the 177th Infantry had never been there.

Aumade concluded with a list, which he asked the Colonel to verify, of the lady acquaintances of Letoque. Throughout, it should be said, the Colonel was most anxious to make clear that his wife was of the same opinion as himself. Aumade thanked him again and ushered him out by a different door from the one through which he had entered.

Mlle Lucille Brassier came next. She was twenty-three, petite, modern and with manners distinctly affected. She announced that she liked Letoque enormously, and it was plain she would have liked to add, in spite of the opinion of her parents. Again Aumade recited the list of friends. And now he ventured to discuss whether any might have been an excellent *partie* for a bachelor like Letoque. One name was particularly prominent— that of a Mme Natalie Perthus, but Lucille was of the amused and even contemptuous opinion that Letoque could never have been enamoured of a frump like her. It was plain indeed that she would go on thinking that the only person of whom he might conceivably have been enamoured was herself.

So much for the stepdaughter of Mme Brassier, but before she herself came in, Aumade had something to reveal. Mme Dubois, that shifty, intriguing housekeeper of Letoque's, had stated in her evidence that on two occasions recently she had been suspicious when her employer had dismissed her for the afternoon, and once—by accident she claimed, though only too obviously by design—she had chanced to see Mme Brassier entering the Villa Sablons by the back door, and she had further found out that at the same time the Colonel and his daughter were at their bathing-hut on the beach.

Mme Brassier, as has been indicated, was the Colonel's second wife. She was a handsome woman of about forty; a brunette with superb eyes and, one would guess, very much of a temper. She was the first of the three to regard with interest and even disquiet the presence of the impassive Gallois and Travers.

She had been perfectly indifferent to Letoque, she said, who had been a friend of very short standing. Aumade, with a special look across at the stenographer, asked if he might put a personal and highly confidential question. Had Letoque ever tried to make love to her?

She drew herself up with a dignity. Was that not in the nature of an insult?

Aumade smiled suavely.

"But no, I assure you. Even to a woman of your honour and standing, it suggests a certain homage."

"I should not have regarded it as homage," she said, but smiled nevertheless.

"And if he had suggested any private visit to him," Aumade went on blandly, "you would have rejected such an invitation with scorn."

"Undoubtedly!" She was looking the least bit uneasy. "Why discuss impossibilities which are also distasteful?"

"Exactly," said Aumade. "But among the ladies of his acquaintance were there any whose ideas were possibly different from your own?"

She shrugged her shoulders. "But I was not interested in his acquaintances."

"Then I will become more personal," Aumade said patiently. "Our evidence shows he was decidedly interested in a certain widow—Mme Perthus."

She smiled with a very definite contempt.

"But Mme Perthus is not the type to interest anybody."

Aumade leaned forward. "You mean, she is not prepossessing?"

She shrugged her shoulders indifferently. "She has admittedly a good figure, but—" Another shrug of the shoulders summed up the rest.

"Ah!" said Aumade as if he understood everything. "And just one other question. You are still positive you were on the veranda when you heard those sounds which might have been the shots?"

"On the veranda, I swear it." Travers and Gallois is exchanged glances at that unnecessary vehemence. "And I knew it was half-past three because in my lap I had the glasses which

I mentioned to you." She smiled sweetly as she once more explained about those. "From the veranda I could see the clock here and I could often make out my husband and Lucille on the beach."

Out went Mme Brassier, the thanks of Aumade in her ears. But no sooner had the door closed than his smile had gone.

"Well, gentlemen, was she his mistress?"

"Undoubtedly," said Gallois. "One would almost say there is no need to look further for the assassin of Letoque. A crime of jealousy perhaps. But there is one question I should like to ask. Have you any more information about this Mme Perthus whose name has already occurred several times?"

"She is a widow, belonging to the Brassier circle," Aumade said. "All our information is that Letoque was on specially good terms with her."

He had pressed the buzzer and now he was speaking. Was there any confirmation about the interview with Mme Perthus? At once a consternation was coming into his tone, and he was asking for Fournal. No sooner had the receiver been replaced than Fournal was coming in. He gave a look of much surprise at the sight of Gallois and Travers.

"What is this about Mme Perthus?" Aumade demanded.

Fournal explained that he had proceeded to her house in order to ensure an interview for two o'clock that afternoon, and had found there was no one there at all. From a neighbouring villa he had ascertained that Mme Perthus had been seen to leave her house on the Tuesday afternoon, and the maid had, it was believed, been sent home on a holiday.

"But," said Fournal with a look of some importance, "I made it my business to discover the gardener, and from him I learned the address of the maid and her name. She is a Marthe Fouré who lives at St. Isare. I returned here therefore to arrange for a car."

"Action is necessary at once," Aumade told him. He glanced at the clock and frowned for a moment in thought. "Inquire at once in the town about this disappearance of Mme Perthus and later perhaps this afternoon you can fetch the woman Fouré."

It was well past noon, but just as they were about to adjourn, in came Briant, the surgeon. Aumade, with whom he appeared to be something of a favourite, introduced him most flatteringly to the two. Gallois liked the look of him at once.

"And the scar?" Aumade asked.

Briant smiled. "It is probably a cut that happened in his youth. Perhaps he fell and tore his knee on some rocks."

"So much for that," said Aumade. "It is only more evidence that he was a liar and a rogue."

After some brief talk, the four parted on the pavement outside the front door. Gallois had requested the pleasure of the company to dinner of both Aumade and the surgeon, but the latter was not free that night and so the dinner was postponed. As for the inquiry, Aumade said he was arranging that afternoon for a test at the Villa Sablons. It was his own opinion the shots could not have been heard from the veranda. After that he did not know what would be happening. Mme Perthus, as he put it, had been one of his trump cards, and now she was missing from the pack.

"Well, is he Bariche?" was Travers's first question as soon as the two had crossed the road.

The smile of Gallois had never been more mournful.

"As the great Shakespeare, says, everything that shines is not the real gold."

"Yes, but what further tests can we apply?"

"That we do not know," said Gallois, and his smile was, if possible, even more melancholy. "Nevertheless there is something that occurs to me. This morning we heard much about women. May we not then arrive at some connection with Rionne?"

"But how?" asked Travers.

"Was it not with a woman that Rionne was seen at Furolles?" Gallois reminded him.

CHAPTER X
A DISCOVERY

CHARLES HAD BEEN so famished after his morning on the beach that he had almost finished his lunch. The hotel was crowded, but Velot had reserved a special table for the three in a corner of the loggia.

"A good appetite is a good sign," said Travers in French. "You're almost yourself again, Charles."

"You will pardon me," said Gallois, "but he will talk in English when with ourselves. By my instruction he continues his studies since you saw him last, and here is an occasion that is admirable for practice. Also there may be times when we do not wish that others understand what it is that we say."

Charles caught the eye of Travers. Travers, older than Gallois, was still, as Charles had come to know, very much of a boy.

"Well then, how are you coming along, Charles?" Travers asked flippantly.

"I come along very well," Charles told him, with a grin. "There is the—the buzz in the head, but very little now."

Gallois nodded benignantly.

"A day or two and he will be able perhaps to assist in this business of Letoque."

"But what has this Letoque to do with Bariche? For my part I do not see a connection."

Gallois gave him a look of sad reproach.

"It appears that this morning you do not rest. On the contrary you occupy yourself with reading the papers."

Charles grimaced. "It is necessary that one passes the time."

Gallois ignored him and turned to Travers. "This afternoon, we will spend on the beach, where I shall perhaps explain this new affair to those who have only read of it in newspapers."

But what he did discuss during lunch was Charles's accident, which, since the Letoque–Bariche discoveries, had acquired in his eyes an even greater significance. Charles was frankly of the opinion of Travers, that the accident was precisely what it had seemed, and that a deliberate collision with his car would have required a timing and an ingenuity which the circumstances could not conceivably have allowed.

Gallois shelved the subject, though far from abandoning his own opinion. After lunch deck–chairs were taken to the beach. It was not too crowded, and there was plenty to observe.

"Lizou would have been an ideal spot for your convalescence, Charles," Travers said. "I wouldn't mind being ill there myself."

"Ah! The country, the mountains, the good air," said Gallois with a grand poetic flourish. "Above all, the quiet, the solitude, in which one can reflect and even create."

Charles once more caught the eye of Travers.

"That is what I thought when I woke," he said in his tentative English. "I ask myself where I am, because everywhere it is quiet. For a moment I tell myself I am dead, because there is no noise even of a *moustique,* but after I have the milk and take a little sleep for an hour I wake again and it is not so quiet—no! There is the noise of sheep and cows, and Gabrielle, she laughs and tells me it is the animals that traverse the road from the fair."

"I met some of them the same night," Travers told him.

Gallois was making a gesture of impatience.

"The sounds of animals are not the noise which yon call them. They also are part of the country." His lip curled. "There are ignorants who say that the chanting of birds is a noise. To them the town. The country should not encumber itself with such imbeciles. But now it is necessary that you rest. Listen, then, while I explain what has arrived concerning this Letoque, about whom you imagine doubtless you have read everything."

"*Parlons français alors,*" Charles told him with a grimace. "*Je suis au bout de mon latin.*"

Travers lay back in his chair and soon the two voices were a peaceful drone that was lulling him to sleep. Then out of the corner of his eye he saw in the distance his old acquaintance the photographer, but as he came nearer, he could see it was not the same one. Then he had an idea.

"I think I'll go along and fetch those photographs," he told Gallois.

Gallois paused in his explanation.

"Obtain also one for this Charles, at my expense. Perhaps one could also arrange that he photographs the three of us, which would be an admirable souvenir for our friends at Lizou."

So through the heat of the afternoon, Travers made his way to the Rue des Alpes and was soon aware of the bay window, which had in it hundreds of photographs. When he walked into the shop, M. Lebrun was busy behind the counter. He smiled at the sight of Travers.

"Good afternoon, sir."

"So you *are* English," Travers said.

"You guessed it then, sir?"

"Yes and no," Travers told him. "What part of England do you come from? London?"

"You've got it first time, sir. Born in Lewisham, and lived there all my life."

Travers was shaking his head and smiling.

"The funny thing is, you know, you look the absolute perfect figure of a Frenchman. And what about the Jaques Lebrun part of it?"

"Well, it's like this, sir. You're not in a hurry by the way? Then we'll go in there. We shall hear the bell if it goes."

They went through to a beautifully fitted studio, where special photographs could be taken if required. Travers took an easy-chair and accepted a cigarette.

"As a matter of fact, sir, my name's Brown—Jack Brown—and I took this French moniker by arrangement. It's like this. My old dad was a photographer, and I went to not a bad sort of school, and as soon as I left I started to help him in the business. Then the war came and I served the last couple of years and ended up on the Rhine. I met a nice little French girl there and married her and took her home with me.

"Then the bottom fell out of the photographic business and we had a pretty tough time scraping along. Then the old dad died and I took over the business, but it wasn't anything much to shout about even then. Then this quick-fire photo business came over from America, and another chap and I tried it out at

Brighton and didn't do so badly. Just as we were going strong along came the depression, so my wife said why shouldn't we come along here to her mother. I spoke French pretty well by then, with what I'd learned at school and what I'd picked up from her, and she reckoned that if we came down here we'd make a packet."

He smiled. "We didn't for a bit, then things picked up, and now we can't grumble. I run another outdoor man and there're a couple of girls working upstairs."

"And now you actually live in Carliens?"

"Most of the year," he said. "We come over in January and stay till September. Then we go back to London where my old mother's still alive."

"Well, jolly good luck to you," said Travers. "As soon as I saw that business card of yours I knew you'd get on."

The bell went, but within a minute or two he was back. Things were always slack in the afternoons, he said. The busiest time was just before lunch and between tea and dinner.

"I expect you've snapped some famous people in your time," Travers said.

He quoted a whole string of them. Of most of the French names Travers was perfectly ignorant.

"And you've had some funny experiences I expect?"

"I have that, sir. I had one only the other day, as a matter of fact." He was frowning in a curiously amused kind of way as he went over to a drawer. "I thought I'd be clever and do some business at that circus which was here the other day."

"I saw it at Furolles," Travers said. "It opened here the same day as I arrived."

"Well, I went along there on the Tuesday morning early. There wasn't anybody at the entrance gate so in I walked. The first one I saw was a young fellow coming my way, and before he could say Jack Robinson I had him, and was giving him my card. Mad? You never saw any one so mad in your life! He spat like a cat and I thought he was going to lay hands on me, and then when he started hollering to a couple of tough-looking blokes and they came running, I started to run first. I don't mind telling you, sir, they didn't see me for dust, and I was behind that mimosa hedge before they knew I'd gone. And then what do you think happened? He came here and asked if I'd actually taken his photograph. I told him I never developed any films which I knew weren't likely to sell. Then he asked if he could buy the film, so I gave it to him to pacify him. I didn't want any trouble with him, though, mind you, he was as different as chalk is from cheese. Butter wouldn't have melted in his mouth. And who do you think he was, sir?"

"Don't know," said Travers.

"Jules Helmont, that trapeze artist of theirs."

"Really? And how did you find out?"

"I've got ways and means," he said. "It was him all right. Have a look at that, sir. Quite a nice-looking fellow, isn't he? Some say he's the son of some big French bug or other, born the wrong side of the blanket."

"But you said you hadn't developed the film."

"You bet your life I developed the film," he said.

Travers polished his glasses and had a good look as it. Then he took it to the window and looked at it again.

"A good-looking fellow, as you say. And what did you actually make of him? I mean what kind of man was he?"

"Oh, he was a gentleman all right, sir, though you wouldn't have guessed it from the sort of job he's doing."

"All work is honourable," Travers told him, and then rather blushed for the sententiousness. "And I suppose if the truth were known he makes as much money a year as either of us."

Then he was getting to his feet. It was much later than he thought, he said, and he would have to be going. As for the third enlargement, he would call for it in a day or so and pay for it with the other two.

Travers got back to the beach to find Charles apparently having a nap and Gallois sitting in profound thought. While he had been going over the case with Charles, he said, new ideas had occurred, and at once he began imparting them to Travers.

"You still wonder perhaps why I refuse to believe that this Letoque is also Bariche, but if I were to believe too soon, and I was wrong, then it would be the tragedy of my life. Also, once more it seems to me that there are instincts which are more important than facts. For example. We assume for a moment that Letoque is Bariche. The history of Bariche is that he is a swindler and a murderer. To kill is essential. It is part of his *metier*—what you call his business. But Letoque is not the murderer. Letoque is a person who is murdered! There is, I think, a difference which demands that we stop and think."

"Yes," said Travers warily.

"If Letoque is Bariche, why is it that Bariche is killed? At once we are requiring a motive, which is also something new."

"I agree to all that," Travers said. "You come down here to discuss perhaps some crime that Bariche had committed or was about to commit, instead of which you find it is Bariche himself who has been killed."

Gallois nodded affably.

"And something else. In a case that has a real importance one is confronted with many clues. But—and it is without doubt the experience of yourself—there is always the clue which has an importance that is supreme. It is the key that unlocks everything. At the moment of your arrival I am demanding of myself if I have in my hands this key, and whether I do not know it."

"I agree," said Travers and smiled dryly. "Unfortunately that kind of key is always the hardest to find."

"Nevertheless, there are things which occur to me," Gallois said gently. "This woman in the hat of black with the white decoration, who was with Rionne at Furolles. It is not impossible that she is Mme Brassier or the Mme Perthus who disappears, and of whom Mme Brassier is so scornful and so jealous."

"You suspect a *crime passionel?*"

"I suspect everything," Gallois said sadly.

Travers was hooking off his glasses.

"Talking of this Mme Perthus, I suppose she cannot already be a victim of Bariche?" Then he smiled feebly. "But of course not. He couldn't have had time to lay hands on her money. But couldn't you find out from her bank whether, for instance, she had realized any securities? That would not only be an indication as to whether she was in the clutches of Letoque, but a real proof that Letoque was Bariche."

Gallois was making a note in his note-book. As soon as possible, he said, it should be done.

"And what of the man who gave to Mme Dubois the free ticket for the circus?"

It was Charles who had spoken. He had been shamming sleep, while he was putting his English words in order. "If he arranges that Letoque should be alone in the Villa that afternoon, why is it not he who kills him?"

"So you do not rest," Gallois told him. "You excite your brain with theories."

"But talking of this man," Travers cut in. "Surely he is a vital factor?"

"Undoubtedly," Charles said. "He is one, for instance, with whom I should like very much to talk."

"In this world, there are many things that one would like," Gallois said with a quiet irony. Then suddenly he paused and the large gentle eyes were turned on Travers. "There is something which you discover?"

"Yes," said Travers, and at once was telling the story of the photographer. Charles made no more pretence of sleep. He sat up and swivelled round in his chair.

"And so this Jules Helmont does not desire to be photographed," was the comment of Gallois. "There is perhaps a truth in the rumours that make of him a man of mystery."

"But wait a minute," Travers said. "I believe when we were coming back from Lizou on that little trip of ours, I pointed out where a young man had taken the wrong road. That man was Jules Helmont. I recognized him from the photograph."

Gallois was trying to be interested, but still did not see the point.

"Think it out for yourself," Travers said patiently. "Just before five o'clock on Monday afternoon last he was at that fork. You were at the circus. Was he at the circus?"

"But yes. I saw him myself."

Travers was slowly shaking his head. "Was it Jules Helmont that you saw?"

Gallois stared. "You mean that there was what you call a—a substitute?"

"Yes. An understudy. And if you remember, Auguste would not climb the rope to a master who was not there. But in the evening, according to the guest at the Hôtel de France who had been there, Auguste performed normally, and therefore the actual Jules Helmont was back again."

The lean fingers of Gallois were feeling the air. "It is this Jules Helmont who gave the ticket to Mme Dubois?"

Travers shrugged his shoulders.

"That may be going too far ahead. Also at the moment, if I were you, I would not show Mme Dubois the photograph. Later we may be able to let her see Jules Helmont himself. But there is another mystery. Auguste, if you remember, was supposed in the afternoon to be sick. In the evening he had recovered. Nevertheless the next day he was dead!"

"Yes," said Gallois. "There were to be no more contretemps like those that I saw at the circus, and therefore he was killed— *ce pauvre Auguste!*"

"That's how I see things myself," Travers said. "But may I suggest something? Why should I not go to-morrow morning to Cannes, or wherever the circus is, and make a few inquiries? Better still, why should not Charles go with me?"

"Charles? But it is impossible. The express orders were that he should rest. One does not go to Cannes with stitches in one's head."

Travers smiled dryly. "I would not take him to Cannes if the stitches were not in his head. But there will be no excitement I assure you. And think. You yourself ought not to leave Carliens at the moment, and at Cannes Helmont will recognize me if he sees me. But nobody connected with the circus has ever seen Charles."

"The night brings counsel," pronounced Gallois, and already it seemed that he was somewhat yielding.

Travers caught the eye of Charles. He, at least, appeared to be having no doubts that the morning would find him on the road to Cannes.

CHAPTER XI
A CRIME OF PASSION?

JUST AFTER five o'clock: Marthe Fouré, the general maid of Mme Perthus, was entering the room of the examining magistrate, She was what one might call a lumpy woman in the thirties, and looked honest, good tempered, and a competent person altogether. She had been at the Villa Vézac with Mme Perthus for four years, and her evidence was this.

Mme Perthus was accustomed to go out a good deal when the weather was congenial, and on the Tuesday morning she was out as usual, though Marthe could not say where. Lunch was always at noon, and just before that time Mme Perthus arrived home, and in a state of considerable agitation. She had had news that an aunt was ill and she would have to go at once. She did not say how she had received the news.

Marthe helped her to pack a bag with enough clothes for at least a fortnight, and this bag Marthe carried— it was all downhill, as she pointed out—to the *autobus* stop beside the Hôtel de la Plage. Madame told her not to wait, so she returned to the Villa before the bus arrived.

The instructions she received were that she was to leave the Villa perfectly tidy and then take a holiday. Madame Perthus thought she might have to stay with this relative for some time, but in a few days she would be sending some news. The other instruction was somewhat unusual. If M. Letoque called before Marthe left the Villa he was to be given the news.

"And her address?" asked Aumade.

"There was nothing about an address," she said. "Mme Perthus told me to say she had no idea when she would be back."

"You did not have to tell M. Letoque that Mme Perthus was going to write to him?"

She shook her head. "No, m'sieu, only what I have told you."

"Did she tell you where she was actually going?" She had given no idea where she was going except that Marthe had assumed that the *autobus* she was taking was going in the direction of Furolles, moreover she had never previously heard her mention any living relative at all.

"And at your home at St. Isare, you received a letter from Mme Perthus?"

"The letter has not yet arrived," she said. "But it does not matter. Madame will send for me as soon as she is back."

"And M. Letoque called before you left the Villa?"

"Oh, yes, m'sieu. He called," she said. "He was very sorry to hear about the relative of Madame and said that doubtless she would write. He was most anxious to know where she was so that he might do something to help."

"M. Letoque was a friend of Madame?" asked Aumade almost jocularly.

"Oh, yes," she said.

Aumade's tone became quite roguish.

"Did you anticipate any outcome of this friendship? A marriage, for instance?"

In her smile there was something that showed she had certainly debated the question in her own mind, and she had doubts—unfortunate doubts.

"M. Letoque was very good-looking," she said. "Madame was very nice, but—"

Aumade nodded sympathetically.

"Well, she might have made him a good wife," he said. "In very strict confidence now, did you think there was anything serious between them?"

She hesitated and looked slightly confused. Aumade repeated the question and the assurance of confidence.

"Well, yes," she said. "Once I saw M. Letoque embrace Madame. It was in the *salon* as I went by the door."

"And Madame was not objecting?"

"She was blushing," said Marthe, and her own round country face was itself one immense blush.

"May I be permitted to ask a question?" said Gallois gently. Marthe was to get on even better with him than with M. Aumade. Perhaps there was something in the mournful poetic smile that appealed to her, for she was obviously romantic at heart.

"You are a most excellent witness," Gallois said, "it is obvious that what you tell us is the truth and that, like ourselves, you have the best interests of your mistress at heart. Now you have assured us that she very often went out, for walks shall we say, or to visit friends."

Marthe smilingly admitted it.

"Then think back to last Thursday week. Was your mistress away that afternoon and did she not return at about six o'clock?"

Marthe made rather heavy going of the question and at last was able to say she was out. Then she was qualifying it at once by adding that almost every afternoon of late she had been out.

"Again in very strict confidence," went on Gallois, "did she ever accompany M. Letoque on those little trips he took in the car to the country?"

Marthe blushingly admitted it.

"And now just one other question," Gallois said. "Madame had a black hat with a white ornament?" He smiled deprecatingly. "Being a man I do not exactly know how to describe this ornament. It was an aigrette perhaps or a flower?"

Marthe believed there was such a hat, but it was not a new one or else she would have remembered it. Also, as she pointed out, most women would have a hat like that.

And that completed the examination of Marthe Fouré.

Aumade announced that the whole party had better proceed at once to the Villa Vézac. He would not have thought of doing so in the absence of Marthe, but said that now she could act on behalf and in the interests of her mistress. Since she had the key she could open the door and discover if any letter had arrived at the Villa.

"You do not think anything has happened to Madame?" asked Marthe agitatedly.

"But no," Aumade assured her. "It is merely that we have some important news for your mistress and naturally we want to discover her whereabouts."

The car that had brought her from St. Isare was waiting and she was asked to take the front seat in order to direct the driver.

The car went almost through the town, then took a sharp right turn and mounted to a quarter that seemed even more select than the Rue des Pins. In less than a minute Marthe was directing the car to halt and there was the Villa Vézac. It seemed a charming little place, its outside spotlessly painted and its little garden beautifully kept.

"Madame has returned!"

No sooner had the eyes of Marthe fallen on the front door than she had stared and now she was running along the path. In the house a woman was pushing aside the fly-net and looking out. Aumade was hurrying forward too, his hat in his hand, but from the background the other two could hear little of the excited explanations. Travers was trying to form some impression of Madame herself. She had a good figure, as even Mme Brassier had conceded, and a pleasant face, but she was fifty if a day, and with what looked like a disfigurement of hair at the corners of her lips and on her chin. Then Gallois was suddenly making a move forward. Mme Perthus seemed to be collapsing, and Marthe and Aumade were supporting her and had disappeared behind the fly-net into the house.

A minute or two and the five were in the *salon*. Mme Perthus was sobbing quietly with Marthe consoling her. The three men stood uneasily by, and not until the sobs at last became spasmodic did Aumade begin to explain.

"Unhappily Mme Perthus has not read the papers and it is only at this moment that she has heard of the tragic death of M. Letoque—a friend she has already learned to respect."

Another minute and she had calmed herself. With profound apologies Aumade asked if he might put a few questions. The assassination of M. Letoque would be avenged by the law, he said, and every friend of the victim was being asked to throw light on the terrible affair.

Mme Perthus was uncommonly informative and helpful, though only, one might have said, in the interests of herself. An aunt had been suddenly taken ill in Toulon and she had been there for a few days. However, the aunt had made an unexpectedly quick recovery, and then she herself had felt homesick and so had come back. She had intended sending for Marthe the same night. As for the tragedy, she was too distressed even to think about it, and she was positive she could give the gentlemen no information at all.

"Then we will intrude no longer," Aumade said. "Once more we offer our apologies and condolences. And this excellent Marthe remains?"

"Of course I remain," Marthe told him.

But as the three were at the car again she all at once came running down the path, and once more her honest country face was blushing as she begged them never to reveal the things she had so loquaciously let fall about her mistress.

Aumade reassured her, and at once she was flying to the house again.

"Quick!" said Gallois as soon as the three were in the car. "Drive at once to telephone headquarters. It is possible that Mme Perthus is already telephoning to this aunt. The conversation should be overheard."

"But if the aunt is not on the 'phone?" asked Aumade, as the car shot on towards the bend.

"Arrange at once for the Villa Vézac to be observed," Gallois said. "If a letter is posted it must be examined."

It was not till Aumade had completed his arrangements that Gallois was able to explain.

"How was it," he said, "that Mme Perthus had heard in Carliens of the illness of a relative in Toulon? She spent the morning out, and it was when she came in that she was suddenly announcing to Marthe that she would have to go at once. Was that announcement made because she had just heard of the death of Rionne? Had she seen one of the photographs that had just been posted? Was there an aunt at all? If so, it seems strange she had never spoken of her to Marthe. Perhaps she had merely been at an hotel and had come back because she had heard of the death of Letoque."

"Possibly it was she who killed Letoque," Aumade said. "She went away to fabricate an alibi."

"It is possible," Gallois said, "but since she has not already telephoned to Toulon there is all the more reason that she should write a letter. If there is a relative she will have to write at once and induce her to agree to that story of a sudden illness."

"And in the morning, if you agree," Gallois went on, "I would like to see the bank manager of Mme Perthus and inquire into her affairs. She looks to me like a woman of too good a heart, and it is possible that Letoque was an adventurer and had designs on her money."

Aumade, looking hastily at his watch, said the idea was an excellent one. But Mme Brassier must have been waiting ten minutes already at the Hôtel de Ville.

"Let her wait," said Gallois. "She is of the type who is likely to be annoyed at being made to wait, and when one is in a temper there are things which are often let fall."

Mme Brassier entered. Aumade was at his desk and he offered no welcoming hand. In the room there was an air of cold legality.

"Sit there, madame, if you please. We hope we shall not detain you long, but it will naturally depend on yourself."

She shrugged her shoulders. Were not the interviews becoming tiresome? Would it not have been possible for them to have asked everything before and got everything over?

"Alas," said Aumade. "From hour to hour various facts keep emerging, and new problems, and we apply to you as the only person who is able to help. But first, to refresh your memory, I will read the previous evidence you have been so good as to give."

Mme Brassier was most uneasy. While listening with a strained attention to the voice of Aumade, she was all the time darting little looks at the two who sat impassively by.

"And now to resume," said Aumade, "On the afternoon of Wednesday, your husband and stepdaughter were bathing. You detest bathing and the noise of the beach, so you remained at the Villa. But you had with you, as usual, the pair of glasses so that you could see the beach and amuse yourself by observing the movements of the bathers."

She gave a somewhat nervous, "Yes."

"You were not in the habit, by any chance, of using those glasses to make sure that your husband and your stepdaughter *were* on the beach?"

Her face flared.

"I do not understand."

Aumade smiled. "Come, madame. Everything said here is in the utmost confidence, and we are all men of the world. I suggest that those glasses were used to make sure that it was perfectly safe for you to visit M. Letoque."

She was springing furiously to her feet. "It's an insult. I demand the protection of my husband."

"Certainly," said Aumade calmly. "If you wish, your husband shall be sent for at once. Meanwhile calm yourself. It is unnecessary to remind you that you are in the presence of the law. But you deny then that you were ever alone with M. Letoque in his villa of an afternoon?"

She had sat down again, bosom heaving. Aumade repeated the question.

"Never," she said. "Again I insist that these are nothing but insults."

Aumade made play with taking up a document from the table and running his eyes carefully over it.

"Nevertheless," he said, "we have a witness who will swear that you were seen to enter his house on two occasions, in the afternoon. If you wish you may be confronted with this witness, but only, of course, in the presence of your husband."

She glared. "It's a lie! Never, never would I do such a thing."

"You wish, then, that we should send for your husband and bring in the witness?"

"No, no!" She was shaking her head and her hands were trembling too. "All the same it is a lie. I swear it."

Once more Aumade shrugged his shoulders.

"But, madame, there are many things which you have sworn. You have sworn, for instance, that it was from your veranda that you heard those sounds that might have been the shots."

There was a quick, wary look at Gallois, then she was moistening her lips.

"But it was on the veranda. I swear it was on the veranda."

Aumade leaned forward.

"This afternoon, as you are aware, certain experiments were conducted at the Villa Sablons and, with the permission of your husband, in your own garden also. Shots were fired from a gun of the same calibre as that which was used to kill Letoque. The experiments proved, beyond doubt, that it was impossible to hear anything from your veranda." He leaned forward again, thrusting out a sudden finger. "The truth, then, or it will be necessary to detain you. The law does not let itself be trifled with. The truth at once!"

She was getting to her feet again. Travers thought she was going to cry, but it was fear that was bringing the shrillness and the hysterics.

"It *is* the truth; I swear I've told you nothing but the truth."

Aumade picked up the receiver, but she was unaware that the buzzer had not been pressed.

"Hallo! Make immediate arrangements please to take Mme Brassier to Toulon, as arranged. Demand the presence of her husband here at once."

There was a shriek as she rushed forward to the table. Aumade rose and confronted her coldly, and his voice had an ironic courtesy.

"There is something you also would like to say?"

She shook her head. Her shoulders all at once drooped.

"You wish to tell the truth?"

"Yes. I will tell the truth."

"Then calm yourself, I beg of you, and sit down."

He was again speaking into the receiver. The arrangements were to be temporarily cancelled.

"So at last we arrive at the truth," he said blandly, "and this time the truth is—what?"

She had visited Letoque, she said, but purely out of friendliness, and she would swear by the Blessed Mother of God there had been nothing dishonourable. That Wednesday afternoon she had wondered casually if Letoque were in, and as she walked round the garden, she went out of curiosity through a gap in the hedge, and it was from there she heard shots, though she did not know they were shots. Nevertheless there was something peculiar about them, and at once she went to the back of the Villa to see if anything was happening there. She was just in time to see someone disappearing among the trees above the path, and she thought it was a man.

"Tell me," said Aumade, "who was it that you expected to see when you went to the back of the Villa?"

Her brain was obviously hunting for some lie, and then as obviously she was deciding to tell the truth.

"It was Mme Perthus," she said. "Once before I saw her enter the Villa by that way."

"Ah!" said Aumade with his usual gasp of satisfaction. "Perhaps after all we are arriving at the truth. And this man that you saw. What was he like?"

But she did not see a man, she said. She had seen a movement of undergrowth and glimpsed someone who might have been either man or woman. That was her story and there was no shaking it. Then she had gone back to the veranda, she said, and looked down to the beach. There was no sign of her husband, and he had spoken of returning early, otherwise she would have gone perhaps to the Villa to confront Letoque.

She seemed surprised when Aumade rose and said the interview was at an end, and there looked like being more hysterics when she refused to sign the statement.

"Sign, madame, sign. The law insists," Aumade told her coldly, and she signed.

"Now you will be conducted back to your house," he told her. "For the moment all this remains secret. You will continue your life in a perfectly normal way, but, nevertheless, you remain at our disposal. One false step and the consequences for yourself may be terrible."

The door closed on her. The room was all at once incredibly empty and incredibly quiet. Aumade leaned back in his chair and mopped his forehead. Travers was shaking his head as he slowly polished his glasses. Never had he heard anything so swift and so terrifying in its deadly coldness.

Aumade let out a breath, "You believe this story, gentlemen?"

Gallois made a gesture of indifference. To him the examination with its drama and even hysterics had been nothing more than the workaday.

"In any case, we are making progress," said Aumade, getting to his feet. "Now we have something definite with which Mme Perthus can be confronted."

"My congratulations," said Gallois, also rising. "What I begin to see emerging from all this is a drama of these two women, and in my opinion it is Mme Perthus who is likely to prove the more interesting,"

Aumade was recovering his papers. At once, he said, he would be preparing for an interview with Mme Perthus, which, unless they heard to the contrary, would be in the morning.

"Unhappily, M. Travers must be absent tomorrow," Gallois said, "and something else I have remembered. M. Travers has, at present, no credentials or authority from yourself. It is not unlikely that a sudden emergency might arise in which he might find it necessary to act."

Aumade was only too pleased to provide the authority. While the credentials were being prepared, he insisted that the two should take an apéritif. Briant, the surgeon, had been present at the experiments that afternoon, he added, and if it was still convenient to Gallois the two would be dining at the Hôtel de France the next night.

*　*　*

As Travers knew, the main reason why Gallois had obtained those credentials was for the proposed visit to Cannes. It was to be Cannes, because just after dinner Gallois had ascertained that the circus was still there, and it was not till the Monday that it was going on to Nice. What Gallois was now wishing to know was what plan of campaign Travers had in mind.

"I think it might be dangerous to approach the management direct," Travers said, "or to try to get hold of Helmont, who seems to be an extraordinarily tough fellow."

Charles said he did not see what could be learned from Helmont. To be absent from the circus was not a crime, and there was nothing to prove that he had given the ticket to Mme Dubois. Even if he had, he might have some excellent reason.

"There is no point in making difficulties," Travers told him, "and one other thing we have got to consider. If Helmont should in any way be implicated in this murder, the circus is getting pretty near the Italian border. Once let him get suspicious and over the border he pops. But what I am proposing to do is to trust to luck. We might get hold of someone connected with the circus and induce him to speak. And what do you think of this?"

It was a large and quite ornate species of visiting-card which he was handing to the astonished Gallois.

Mr. L. Travers,
Imperial Circuses Ltd.,
London

Head Office,
St. Martin's chambers, W.C.2

"I ordered that as a rush job from a local printer as soon as I left that photographer," Travers told him. "I shall represent this imaginary circus, and Charles shall be my interpreter. Ostensibly, I shall be trying to sign up acts for my Christmas season in London."

Gallois said the scheme promised well, and he had every confidence in Travers.

"All these trapezists puzzle me," he said. "Why is it necessary for them to wear the masks?"

"Possibly there is some truth in the rumours," Travers said. "It might be dangerous for them to be recognized."

Gallois was most sceptical.

"To you the photographer announced that this Helmont is the illegitimate son of some personage, and therefore he is masked, but the women cannot be illegitimate daughters also unless this personage was a performer on a grand scale. If this Helmont is a Russian prince, then why must he hide his face? In France there are thousands of White Russians."

"There is something which occurs to me," Charles said, and then grinned. "Doubtless it is something which does not occur to any one else. It is that we are mistaken about Letoque. It is not he, but Helmont, who is Bariche."

"On the contrary," pointed out Travers. "Helmont is not a day over thirty-five, and I'd swear his hair is genuinely dark."

"Nevertheless it is curious how Bariche was connected with circuses." He made a gesture of impatience. "That is not the word that I wish. *Il était fou des cirques.*"

"To be mad about circuses, or as one says in English, to be a fan of the circus, is not to say that Bariche was ever an artist," Gallois told him, and then was getting to his feet.

All had a long day before, them, he said, and for M. Travers he counselled bed. In the case of Charles he insisted on it.

CHAPTER XII
GALLOIS IS CONVINCED

Coffee was early and everything was ready at half-past eight. Charles said he was feeling perfectly fit again, with not even a buzz in the head. Nevertheless Gallois insisted there should be no excitements, and as the car moved off a stranger would have guessed from the gentle sadness of his smile that Charles was departing for some distant and dangerous region from which he was scarcely expected to return, But free from the overwhelming presence of his chief, Charles was in great form; alert to point out this and that, interested in the running of the car and, as they drew near Cannes, fertile in suggestions for the handling of the enterprise.

"In a famous English cookery-book," Travers told him, "there is a remark that before you cook a hare—un lièvre—you must catch this hare. Perhaps we might begin therefore by catching our circus."

The circus turned out to be not in Cannes, but half-way between Cannes and Juan les Pins, an admirable arrangement from a business point of view. From the road it was soon recognized, and Travers slowed down the car and crawled by to reconnoitre. Then a van suddenly emerged from the entrance. It was a small one of the type used by bill-stickers with an extending ladder fastened to the back, and it was off in the direction of Nice. Travers was following at once.

It was rather tricky work. Snorting like a hornet the little van dodged its way in and out of the traffic of Antibes, and then it took curves at a speed which threatened to capsize it, and was dodging and twisting again on the outskirts of Nice. In the very middle of the Promenade des Anglais it turned as if making for Cimiez, only to pull up with practically no warning in front of a shop in a side street. To avoid an accident Travers had to go twenty yards past it before bringing his own car to a halt.

"A man is getting out," announced Charles, and then before he could say another word the van was shooting on again. It snorted, passed the Rolls, was on to the corner, and with a whirl of dust was out of sight.

"And now what?" said Travers, feeling very much in a dilemma.

"The man is going into the shop," Charles said.

"Then get out and have a look," Travers told him. "If necessary go into the shop and buy something."

Charles was back almost at once. The shop was acting as a temporary agency for the sale of circus tickets, and the man who had come from the circus was probably checking up sales in readiness for the arrival of the circus on the following day. The van had probably gone on well ahead to post the bills.

Travers moved the car on, reversed, and came back with the agency under observation, and all the time he was rehearsing with Charles just what should be done.

"The man looked as if he might be amenable," Charles said.

It was half an hour before the door opened and he came out. He looked something like a far from prosperous clerk, and about forty, and as he turned to make for the Promenade des Anglais, Charles overtook him. Soon there was much gesticulating and shrugging of shoulders, and waving back at the car, and then the man appeared to see the point that Charles had been trying to make, Travers leaped out of the car at once. Two minutes later the three were under the pleasant shade of an awning waiting for drinks to arrive, and the man— Floc was his name—was trying to make sense out of the card which Travers had handed to Charles and Charles had ceremoniously passed on.

The drinks arrived, and Charles was at once voluble—so much so in fact that Travers was far from following all he said. But he did gather that Charles was stating that in addition to being secretary and interpreter for *M. le patron* when in France, he himself was also an artist of some repute. Travers took out his wallet and removed some notes.

"I myself speak a certain amount of French," he said, making that French none too good. "It is not very good French and— well—*il faut améliorer mon accent.*"

"But the gentleman speaks very good French," said Floc. "Provided one can make oneself understood, that is all that one wants."

"If you do not understand, my secretary, M. Rabaud, will explain," stated Travers. "What I am looking for is trapeze acts, and I am especially interested in the Troupe Helmont. The English love animals, and there is money, I believe, in Auguste, the rat which I saw for myself at Furolles."

"But Auguste is dead!"

Travers was suitably stupefied. Charles threw his hands to heaven, and said it was a pity there had been a waste of time.

And then Floc perhaps was beginning to be suspicious that all was not what it seemed. If the English gentleman had seen the circus at Furolles, why had he not approached the troupe there and direct? The fertile Charles cut in at once.

"At that moment we were not in need of trapezists. We had already engaged an American Troupe, the Troupe Boston, of whom you have certainly heard. Then yesterday we received a cable that unfortunately one of them had died, and that is the reason we are here now, *M. le patron* does not expect information for nothing, even if it is absolutely confidential and between ourselves."

Travers took the hint and passed over a five-hundred-franc note, Floc expressed himself as only too delighted to give any information.

"I admit," said Travers, "that the death of the rat is a blow to me. It lowers pretty considerably the value of the act. How did he die? Was it an accident?"

"Wait a minute," said Charles. "Yesterday when we were inquiring about this Troupe Helmont, did not someone tell us that the rat had been ill?"

Floc said that had been all *blague*. What had happened was this. Auguste belonged to M. Helmont who trained him himself, but there were occasions when M. Helmont was unwell, or perhaps temperamental even, and then understudy took his place and the act was considerably modified, but the management did not wish the audience to know that the understudy was performing, and so M. Helmont had been training Auguste to get used to the understudy and thought he had succeeded, The first time they tried him out, which was at Carliens, there had been a contretemps, followed later by an angry scene between Helmont and Signor Pertini. Pertini was most annoyed but had not dared to say too much, The contract of the Troupe expired on the 30th April, and he was hopeful of engaging them again, for they were undoubtedly an enormous attraction. The next morning Auguste was found dead in his cage and Helmont was overcome by grief. He even accused Pertini of being concerned.

Travers had been shaking his head. "'This business of temperament is difficult, or of loss of nerves. I could engage the understudy, but that increases expense, it occurs often?"

The understudy had been engaged in Paris as a necessary precaution, Floc said, and it was usual in that sort of act. Charles objected. Floc instead. A heated argument began and Travers had to intervene. Floc resumed.

In Paris the understudy performed occasionally as a matter of routine, and also on the journey down to the South. At Carliens, however, Helmont. had said he was feeling particularly nervy, and it would be dangerous for himself to perform, and it was the understudy who did perform practically all the time.

"He is a man of quick temper, this Helmont?"

Floc said he might have given a wrong impression. Helmont was a gentleman, and easy enough to work with. There wouldn't have been a quarrel at all except for Pertini's already having a grievance over something that had happened at Furolles. Just when the act was about to begin Helmont had disappeared. They hunted everywhere for him with all the audience waiting, and then when he turned up he said he had recognized some old friends and had had to speak to them.

"Well, everything requires thought," Travers said, and was fingering a thousand-franc note. "All this conversation is very confidential. If Helmont knew of it he would think I wanted him badly, and the price would go up. And I must admit the death of this Auguste has made a great difference."

"Beggars cannot be choosers," cut in Charles. Travers shrugged his shoulders.

"Nevertheless, I must think things out. If I am of the same mind then as I am now, I may engage this troupe just before their contract ends. Meanwhile if anything happens, perhaps you will have the goodness to inform me at once. For a few days I am staying with friends at Carliens at the Hôtel de France."

He wrote the address and handed it over together with a thousand-franc note, Floc was naturally gratified. He had picked up ten pounds in not much more than, ten minutes, and there was a very excellent promise of more to come. So he began praising the troupe. They were a very great draw and a very fine act. The understudy, in his opinion, was as good as Helmont himself.

"What nationality is this, Helmont?" Travers asked.

"French. The other two are sisters and really are Helmont. They were with the Cirque Fleishmann in Berlin for two years till Jeanne had her accident."

"You mean, during the act?"

"No, she was passing a leopard's cage and her face was torn. That is why all the troupe wear masks, for one side of her face is absolutely hideous."

"But what excellent publicity!" said Travers. "And do the management spread rumours about their nationality for the purpose of more publicity?"

"Exactly. It is something, m'sieu, I would recommend for yourself if you should decide to engage them."

"Find the real name of this Helmont?"

Floc shrugged his shoulders, "In the circus his name is Helmont, It is the business of nobody if he has another name."

That was virtually all.

Floc said he was returning by the van which was due now at any time. Travers repeated the necessity for the strictest confidence.

"There is a matinee this afternoon?" asked Charles.

There was, Floc said, at the usual time.

So much for that. Travers was of the opinion that it was the circus, as such, in which Charles was interested, rather than the inquiry, but he had to admit to himself that another visit might not be waste of time, And in some of the time that remained on their hands he rang Gallois at Carliens and gave him a tough outline of the morning's happenings. Gallois naturally seemed disappointed, for interesting as some disclosures had been, from the point of view of the inquiry they were decidedly negative. Gallois himself had developments at Carliens and he reminded Travers not to be late, and that Aumade and the surgeon were due for dinner unless anything unexpected happened.

They were not unimportant those developments which Gallois had mentioned. When he arrived at the Hôtel de Ville, Aumade had hailed him with congratulations. The deductions about Mme Perthus had been correct. A letter had been sent to the relative in Toulon and it had been opened and sealed again. Its contents appeared to be absolutely damning. The relative was not an aunt but a cousin, and she was asked as a matter of great urgency and secrecy to agree to be referred to as an aunt, and she was to pretend she had been unwell. The letter said there were private reasons which would be explained later by the sender, personally.

With regard to that last Aumade had still further news. That very morning Mme Perthus had taken the *autobus* for, apparently, Toulon, where she was being followed.

Gallois offered congratulations of his own.

"And when are you going to confront this Mme Perthus?" he said.

"There is no hurry," Aumade told him. "When we swoop it must be absolutely unexpectedly. She must be so taken by surprise that she will be unable to keep back a single word of the truth."

The two went on to the bank and there interviewed the manager. His disclosures were even more interesting, Mme Perthus, whose late husband, by the way, had been a silk factor at Lyons, had asked him to realize certain securities, amounting to over a thousand pounds. He advised her that values had fallen, but in his opinion were due for a rise, and he therefore counselled delay. At the same time Mme Perthus hinted that she was likely to be leaving Carliens in the not too distant future. Two days later she telephoned implicit instructions to sell, although he again advised her to wait a few days. He therefore sold and she was notified that the cash was at the bank.

That was all he had heard until the Thursday afternoon before Good Friday, though in the meantime transfers had been sent to her for signature. On that Thursday afternoon she telephoned that she had changed her mind and would he at once be prepared to advise her about reinvestment of the cash.

"And from where was she telephoning?" asked Aumade.

"From her house, I presume," said the manager, somewhat surprised. "There was no indication that she was telephoning from anywhere else."

The two made their way back to the Hõtel de Ville. Everything, as Aumade said, was now becoming clear. Letoque was one of those scoundrels like the late unspeakable Bariche who preyed upon women. If he had not been killed he would already have departed with Mme Perthus and her money, and he would have bled her till she had never a sou left.

Gallois expressed himself as quite in agreement. If only to conceal the elation which he felt he even assisted Aumade in drawing up those direct and terrifying questions which at the right moment should he hurled at the astounded Mme Perthus. Before he left for lunch word came that she had taken the Toulon *autobus* for Carliens again. As far as Gallois was concerned the day's inquiries ended. That afternoon he wrote his notes on the case, and long before the time for dinner had changed his clothes and had gone into the details of the menu with Velot, and chosen the wines. When Travers arrived he sat in his bedroom while he dressed.

Aumade and Briant were on time, and what happened at that dinner is of no particular account. It was an excellent one, the wines were good and Velot himself saw that the service was perfect. Afterwards the four played French billiards while Travers watched, and then they yarned away for an hour, by which time it was ten o'clock and M. Aumade was rising to go. Then came the chance word.

"I suppose nothing else peculiar has turned up about that scoundrel Letoque?" Gallois happened to ask Briant as they stood for a last minute on the hotel steps.

"I meant to tell you," Briant said. "A most interesting thing has happened, at least from a professional point of view, I needn't tell you that hair grows to a minute extent after death. Well, I just happened to be having a look at his scalp and I noticed the original fair hair that had just pushed through underneath the dyed. Then I noticed a most extraordinary thing. There was quite a big patch on the cheek where the hair was a slightly different colour. It had a very faint reddish tinge, in fact. Naturally I had another good look, and what do you think? I found there was a palm of new skin as big as the palm of my hand."

"New skin?" said Gallois somewhat puzzled.

"Yes, new skin had been grafted on his cheek. There is practically no limit to the amount one can graft. When I came to have a really good look, of course, I could see the scars underneath the hair."

Gallois did his best to speak calmly. "It was an old operation?"

"Oh, no. I should say it had been done in the last few months."

He went on to give an experience of grafting when the wrong skin had been chosen for the nose of a patient, and subsequently hair, much to the patient's embarrassment, began growing on the nose. However, he was recompensed by a considerable sum obtained in the courts.

Aumade was highly amused at that anecdote. Gallois waited impatiently for his chuckles to subside. Briant came in with a fatal comment.

"It's by no means an uncommon mistake," he said. "All the same the whole thing, however interesting it may be to me professionally, shows precisely why Letoque grew a beard and then dyed it."

"And what might have caused the original wound that made the grafting necessary?" Gallois asked.

"One cannot say for a certainty," Briant told him. "In all probability it was a burn. I thought I could detect faint traces."

Another minute and the final good-nights were over. Gallois lingered on the steps. His eyes rose to the clear heaven with its innumerable stars. Then he was shaking his head and his hand went out to Travers.

"Thanks to you, my friend, there is no longer doubt. This Letoque is Bariche, and you will be able with a good conscience to relate the history to your grandchildren."

Travels smiled. "Not thanks to me. It's Briant we have to thank."

"And it is I who should have known," Gallois said. His shoulders rose and his palms spread in humiliation. "I am the imbecile. Everything under the nose and I announce that this Rionne is a nobody—an unimportant who is not worth the attention of me, Gallois."

Travers shook his head again.

"In another day or two you will be back in Paris and saying to certain gentlemen, "Messieurs, this Bariche was not only a murderer, and a robber of women, he was also a magician, He burned himself to death at Auteuil and now, six months later, he has contrived to have someone else blow out his brains at Carliens!"

Gallois was patting Travers on the shoulder and smiling with a mournful anticipation.

"Yes" he said, and all at once was taking Travers's arm. "And now, my friend, we arrange at once our own inquiries for to-morrow. Two days perhaps, as you say, and we complete for the last time the dossier of Bariche."

CHAPTER XIII
TREASURE TROVE

COFFEE HAD BEEN ordered early for that morning. Charles was anxious to lend a hand in the day's inquiries, for he was no longer appreciating a convalescence which, in fact, had ceased to exist. But Gallois was adamant. When he was of the age of Charles, he said, he would never have ventured to thrust himself in upon the decision of his superiors. Travers listened amusedly to their arguments. To one like himself who knew the whole history of Charles, there was always a joy in the brief squabbles, though it was Charles who was the main amusement, with his shrewd discernment of when to be the deferential subordinate and when the adopted son.

"You will remain here and continue to rest," was the last word of Gallois.

"Then I shall swim," said Charles.

Gallois made a gesture of indifference. "If you wish to excite yourself contrary to the orders of the doctor, it is your affair. The cemeteries are full of such."

"Then I shall write a letter to Dr. Debran and Gabrielle," Charles said, and, with a quick look at Travers, "unless you, yourself, have already written as you promised."

Gallois looked about to explode with exasperation. Travers cut in quickly.

"Write your letter by all means, Charles, and send our very best wishes. But you cannot post the letter here. We are supposed to be at Mariette and Gabrielle would feel very badly hurt. And what about those stitches in that head of yours?"

Charles said they were of no consequence. Dr. Debran had told him that they could be removed in a week or ten days.

Gallois was impatient to be off, and it was to the Hôtel du Sud that he and Travers made their way. Travers, who knew the waiter, was to do the talking. It was the proprietor, however, a M. Cabon, whom they happened to see first. Travers said they had come in the matter of Rionne. First as to his voice.

"A peculiar sort of voice," Cabon said after considerable thought.

"You will pardon me," broke in Gallois, "but was it anything like this?"

The imitation he gave quite astonished his hearer.

"Then you knew this M. Rionne?" he said.

"Yes," said Gallois off-handedly. "But now we want to obtain some information that requires absolute accuracy—the movements of Rionne last Tuesday week."

Cabon gasped. The gentleman was asking the impossible.

A couple of minutes later there was a miniature conference in the dining-room. An elderly *domestique* was there, a boy, Cabon himself and the waiter. A hubbub of argument and there emerged the fact that on that Tuesday M. Rionne for the first and only time had been late for his dinner. He arrived home at nine o'clock and announced that he had already dined. And nine o'clock, as Gallois knew, coincided with the arrival at Carliens of the *autobus* from Toulon.

"And now on the Thursday," he said. "Two days, that is, after that Tuesday."

But another minute or two of hubbub produced nothing except the certainty that Rionne had spent the afternoon out of the hotel, which in fine weather was his usual practice. Gallois, who still had another string to his bow, expressed his satisfaction. A tip of appreciation was bestowed on the staff.

"And where now?" asked Travers. "Furolles?"

"One moment," Gallois told him. "There are difficulties. We arrive at a time when it requires an agility to keep this Bariche to ourselves. If we interview M. Cippe and obtain perhaps information, then consider what might happen. M. Aumade decides for reasons of his own to bring Cippe here and question him, and you and I are at the examination. He observes us—this Cippe— and remarks that he has already given us the information which M. Aumade demands. Then M. Aumade says to himself, 'What is this? Things arrange themselves behind my back.'"

"Then why not go and see Aumade now?" suggested Travers. "Say there ought to be absolute certainty that Rionne was at Furolles, and since you have discovered his peculiar voice, you have only to ring Cippe and he should be able to give you that final proof."

Half an hour later Gallois joined Travers and Charles on the beach. The voice had been verified by Cippe, he said, and Aumade had at the same time arranged that Cippe was to be present that afternoon at the preliminary examination of Mme Perthus.

"He hinted also a surprise which he keeps, as you say, up the sleeve," Gallois said. "The afternoon promises indeed an amusement, and it is with regret to us, my dear Charles, that you will not be able to observe the excellent methods of our friend Aumade. But now we arrange our information."

All the next hour Travers kept thinking that the three were like adventurers who had hunted for treasure and unearthed it. Now it was as if they were in some lonely spot and examining each item with gloating eyes and caressing fingers. And the pick of the treasure and the most miraculous find of all was the fact that the informer, though no priest, had been discovered.

Gallois with almost a solemnity was writing in his notebook the sequence of events, some undoubted facts and some never to be proved. First there was Bariche who, having left a corpse for himself, made his doubtless prearranged way to Switzerland with the money of his latest victim. But in lighting the fire which ought to have entirely wiped out the Auteuil villa, he received a nasty burn on the face which would not only make him a marked man for life, but would put a very definite end to his highly profitable Bluebeard career. But then he ran up against Rionne. Skin was grafted and time was left for the scars to heal and the beard to grow before Bariche set out to resume in France his profitable career.

What Charles suggested was that Bariche had swindled Rionne out of the proposed fee for the operation, for practically no money had been in the possession of Rionne at his death. A man of the cold-blooded and murderous treachery of Bariche would not have thought twice about a swindle of that sort, and then Rionne, with his special knowledge as a surgeon, then or previously, put two and two together, and either from the newspaper description or from what Bariche himself had chanced to reveal, had formed the opinion that his swindling patient was either Bariche or someone very much like him. Then he had the good luck to spot him in Carliens. He was hard up and he decided to get his own back with interest.

But it was not professional etiquette that made Rionne hesitate about an open personal denunciation of Bariche. Like Bariche, Rionne himself had very few scruples. His primary concern was that in making the revelation his own record should not be unearthed by the police. Therefore he was going to induce a third party to make the disclosures and then collect the reward himself, probably insisting on cash. That third party was undoubtedly the woman with whom he was discussing his plans in Cippe's restaurant at Furolles. As for his choice of the Syndicat building in Toulon for the rendezvous, that now appeared natural. Rionne was probably a stranger in Toulon. He would have gone to the Syndicat d'Initiative for information and it would have struck him as an excellent place at which to meet Gallois.

Now how had Rionne become aware of the woman, and the desirability and likelihood of her co-operation with himself? Only by spying on Bariche as soon as his preliminary plans were made. And who was the woman? Doubtless either Mme Perthus or Mme Brassier, with enormous odds on the former. And what did he tell her? He gave her vague hints perhaps that Letoque was not all he seemed and gradually led up to the supposedly dead Bariche, and so to a sudden fearful terror in her mind. There would be a proof he could suggest to her. The dyed hair was a minor one and she could watch his reactions if she refused after all to realize her securities and to leave Carliens.

But the chief thing was that either by chance or because his spyings were not sufficiently guarded, Letoque himself had spotted Rionne. Then there was a game of the watcher being watched, and it was Rionne who ended up with a knife in his back. Mme Perthus heard the news next morning and at once must have been in a condition that was almost beyond panic. She must have guessed that all that Rionne told her was the truth and at once she was fleeing to Toulon where Letoque should never again clap eyes on her. Then she read the news of his death and the same day was indiscreet enough to telephone her bank manager that she had changed her mind about her securities.

"To complete the dossier there remains one thing," Gallois said, and his knuckles rapped the note-book. "Here we shall write down the name of the killer of Bariche. That alone is necessary to vindicate myself in Paris."

Travers was suddenly frowning. Surely the dossier could never be really completed unless Aumade knew the whole truth? After all he was in charge of the inquiry into the murders of both men. And that was a prospect which Gallois was finding decidedly unattractive. Having begun with necessary prevarication and concealment, he would cut a remarkably poor figure in the eyes of Aumade if the whole truth had finally to come out.

"You will pardon the suggestion," said Charles in his careful English, "but *is* it our affair to discover who it was that killed Bariche? Is it not sufficient for you to prove to certain ones in Paris that what they pleased to call fantastic was after all the truth?"

Gallois looked horrified. His hands rose quiveringly, then fell. The eyes that he turned on Travers were full of pain.

"Consider this Charles. Him I endeavour to make a someone. Now I demand of you, where is the honour and the pride?" Then he was whipping round at Charles. "So, what you once begin it is not necessary to finish. You leave things in the air because perhaps you desire yourself to return to Paris." He made a gesture of the profoundest contempt. "You, if you wish, return to Paris and leave this country of which you have already expressed a distaste. For me there remains the assassin of Bariche. *Moi, je suis Gallois. Je reste.*"

"*Et moi, aussi,*" said the unruffled Charles. "*Tout de même—*" He broke off. "Nevertheless as one says in English, he is not an assassin, this one who kills Bariche. He does not merit the guillotine. He merits instead the reward for which Rionne was himself so anxious."

"For my part," said Gallois with enormous patience, "I am two men, but two men who do not make intrusion upon themselves. When I am a philosopher I am not the law, and when I am the law I am not a philosopher or indeed a philanthrope. At the moment I am Gallois and I demand the assassin, no matter who that assassin is."

The shrug of Charles's shoulders admitted all that. Nevertheless, he said, it was a problem that sooner or later would present itself to the law. Suppose, for example, he himself, or even M. Travers, had killed Bariche. Then what would be the views of Gallois on the matter?

"*Parlous d'autre chose,*" Gallois told him with cold finality. Travers once more cut placatingly in.

"Enough of the present. Why not celebrate the past and drink to the future?"

In a couple of minutes the three were at a table on the veranda of the hotel. The clouds had gone from the brow of Gallois and he was his old mournful self again.

* * *

Two o'clock came, which was the hour for the examination of the widow, Natalie Perthus. There were to be tremendous surprises, the chief of which was the enormous change in her attitude. The previous afternoon on her return to the Villa Vézac she had avoided awkward questioning by taking refuge in tears. Now, while still somewhat nervous, she was a woman with a story that had been well rehearsed.

Aumade had anticipated a most profitable afternoon. He would ask her how she came to have discovered in Carliens that morning that the aunt at Toulon was ill. Then having received that repetition of false information he proposed to tell her with all the terrifying accompaniment of mystery just what she had written to that relative. Then, of course, would come the old game of threats of arrest only to be avoided by a complete confession and the absolute truth.

But all his guns were spiked well ahead, and Aumade himself was to some extent responsible, for the specious courtesy and warmth of his greeting and his renewed sympathies made Mme Perthus at once lose much of the nervousness that she had felt on entering the room. She had something to confess, she said, and she hoped she might be forgiven. In the stress of the previous afternoon she had given wrong information and she had been ashamed of herself ever since. The truth was this. She had all at once grown tired of Carliens and on that Tuesday morning made up her mind to spend a few days in Toulon with her relative. But Marthe was always exasperatingly curious and began asking if the relative was ill, and out of annoyance she had fed the curiosity with anything that occurred on the spur of the moment. But once she had let Marthe imagine she was going to a sick aunt, the same story had to be repeated on the return in the presence of both Marthe and the police.

"Then," said Mme Perthus, "I was afraid of what I had told the police, who might perhaps find out it was a lie, so I wrote a letter to my cousin asking her to support me in this lie, but my cousin, who is a good woman and very scrupulous by nature, insisted that I confess the truth."

So flabbergasted was Aumade that all he could do was to stammer a mild reprimand for the deception. But the biggest of his guns to be spiked was the cousin herself, who had been brought from Toulon and was waiting in the adjoining room for the anticipated confrontation. Something, he knew, had gone badly wrong. The letter that had been opened must have been clumsily resealed. The two women had had their suspicions and had concocted their story.

"We will leave it at that," he said. "Will you inform us, however, of the exact relationship between yourself and M. Gustave Rionne?"

She was wary at once and leaned forward with a curious gesture of deafness.

Aumade repeated the question and she shook her head.

"I have never heard of this M. Rionne."

"As you wish," said Aumade with a slight impatience. "But will you tell us your exact whereabouts on the afternoon of last Thursday week?"

A kind of tranquillity came over her at once, though she had to frown in thought before she could suddenly remember. Thursday week was a long time ago and yet—of course!—she had spent the afternoon with her cousin at Toulon.

"Then perhaps someone was impersonating you," Aumade said ironically. "Unless perhaps you got off the *autobus* at Furolles and waited there. We have here, for instance, a gentleman who claims to have seen you that afternoon at Furolles."

"But it is impossible," she said.

"Nevertheless you will permit that we bring in this gentleman?" said Aumade, and almost at once Cippe was in the room.

"Have you ever seen this lady before?" he was asked.

Cippe looked, looked again and then was shaking his head.

"Have the goodness to stand, madame," Aumade said.

But Cippe had seen enough. It was not the lady he said, and if madame would pardon the remark, it had been a much younger lady than herself.

Gallois was smiling ironically. The veil that Mme Perthus had worn at Furolles had magnificently performed its work. Aumade should have made her dress as she had been at Furolles, and the last thing Cippe should have been allowed to see was her face.

Aumade, still not without hope, began asking about the relationships between herself and Letoque. He had been merely a friend, she said, though a very kind friend, and when questioned she admitted that he had proposed marriage and she herself had toyed with the idea.

"But at my age one does not marry again without a great deal of consideration," she said. "Also I have no illusions about myself."

So much for Mme Perthus. So exasperated was Aumade that he omitted to give the usual thanks and it was with something of an acerbity that he warned her to hold herself at the disposal of the authorities. The door closed on her and he could express his feelings.

"It is inexplicable," he said, and his hands quivered as he raised them. "Everything has been anticipated."

Then he was using much the same words as Gallois had used that morning to Travers when discussing whether the accident to Charles had really been an accident after all. It was, he said, as if Mme Perthus had involved herself in a whole series of sinister happenings, which perhaps were going on around them still, and of which they knew nothing. He himself had a feeling of being in an atmosphere of alarm which recalled that time in the Great War when beneath his feet he had heard faint sounds and knew that somewhere below was an enemy mine.

Gallois gave a mournful shake of the head and committed himself to nothing. Travers asked if anything had been discovered about that cousin at Toulon.

Aumade revealed that she was present and was ordering at once that she should be brought in. She was a spinster, he said, and her name was Vincent.

At the very first sight of her Gallois stirred with an interest. She was a woman of the age of Mme Perthus, but gaunt and thin lipped. Her small close-set eyes were coldly watchful and her face had the yellowish paleness of a nunnery. Her clothes were black and a religious medal hung from a thin silver chain around her neck.

Her voice had a monotony behind which was a vicious calculating brain. What she said in that room does not matter except that she verified in each detail the evidence of her cousin, and when she had gone there was on uneasy quiet as though the room had been relieved of the presence of something chill and malignant. It was a moment or two before Aumade could speak, and again he was making a gesture of helplessness.

"These women baffle me," he said, and again his hands were raised quiveringly to heaven. "It is perjury. Lies—nothing but lies! And yet, how can we prove it?"

Gallois shook a sympathetic head. "If these women have made up their minds to commit perjury, then you are helpless. As for this Vincent, there is no doubt whatever that she has been bribed. If necessary others will be bribed." He smiled ironically. "Mme Perthus has made an alliance with a viper and that viper will not be afraid to sting."

"Yes," said Travers with a considerable disquietude. "That cousin holds her in her hand, like this. If Mme Perthus has been forced to make her her heiress, then in my opinion Mme Perthus is not very long for this world."

"There are methods of dealing with vipers," said Aumade grimly. "But about the conduct of this investigation what do you advise?"

"One might try to create discord between the two," Gallois said. "In a case like this everything is legitimate. Tell one of them that the other has said this, and out of that you will find something to tell the other. That might make a crack into which you can insert your lever. Then at last you may have them accusing each other of perjury."

"A slow business," said Aumade with a gloomy shake of the head, and Gallois wondered if he was thinking about his vines.

"And there is Mme Brassier," went on Gallois. "She also might be confronted with Mme Perthus. There will be recriminations and accusations and something is bound to be let fall."

Aumade nodded once or twice then was getting to his feet. Gallois proffered the hand of sympathy.

"Notify us at once," he said, "when you need our services. Meanwhile if there is any action which it seems to us we might take without first consulting with yourself, will you give us permission? There is Mme Dubois, for instance, with whom I would like to have something of a private talk."

Aumade not only gave permission but made something like entreaty. And so ended that early evening. Gallois, as he walked back to the hotel, could comment with a cynical relief.

"Our good friend Aumade has had an experience which is unusual for himself," he said. "All the time this Perthus tells her admirable story I say to myself, 'Alas, my poor Aumade, you now experience what I myself experienced for months when the relative of the victims of Bariche preferred to say nothing and would make martyrs of themselves in order to conceal that they were the dupes of one so devilish as Bariche.' I tell myself that here again is a woman who will never announce to the world that she has been a dupe and make of herself a public scandal. Rather than make admission even in confidence she pays an enormous price. She places herself at the mercy of this boa constrictor, this Vincent, who will squeeze and squeeze until this Mme Perthus is only a pulp."

Then he shrugged his shoulders.

"But that is not our affair. That is the affair of our poor Aumade. Now he will have his hands full of inquiries; interrogations out of which will arrive—nothing. As for us, we still keep Bariche to ourselves."

A faint uneasiness came over Travers, as it always did, at these glimpses of the ruthlessness in Gallois.

"Yes," he said, "for the moment there is no need to tell Aumade about Bariche. But what was that special reference you made to Mme Dubois?"

"At once," said Gallois, "we take her to the bureau of the photographer and show her that photograph of Jules Helmont. After that it is not impossible that to-night we should sleep at Cannes."

CHAPTER XIV
GALLOIS IS CARELESS

OVER AN APÉRITIF the two had a quick conference, preparatory to that interview with Mme Dubois.

It was a pity, Gallois said, that the matter of Jules Helmont had not been gone into before. Not that he had ever lost sight of it, but it had been Aumade who had dictated the course of the inquiry, and Aumade knew nothing whatever about the trapezist and the curious affair of Auguste, the little climbing rat. Fournal had been sent to the circus on the off—chance of finding the person who had given the free ticket, and it was a hundred to one against his ever having clapped eyes on Helmont at all.

"Whoever it was that gave the Dubois woman the ticket, I cannot fit him in," Travers said. "Call him X for convenience. Did X arrange for Letoque to be alone so that X could kill him, or was X the agent of a third person? As far as I'm concerned that seems the really vital clue."

Gallois shrugged his shoulders.

"If X himself killed Letoque what was the motive?" went on Travers. "Are we to go back to that original idea of both Rionne and Letoque being connected with that dope gang in Switzerland, and was X therefore the emissary sent to get rid of them both?"

"All these problems I also consider," said Gallois, "and therefore I wish to see this Dubois. If she does not recognize the photograph of Helmont, then perhaps it will be as you say. If she says that here is the man who gave her the ticket, then we arrive at something which is more a mystery than before. Why should this trapezist, this Helmont, kill Letoque? For months he is with the circus. It cannot be that he is an emissary sent from Switzerland."

"Well," said Travers, "after Mme Dubois has seen the photograph we shall have two perfectly clear courses open to us. If she recognizes Helmont, then we go and see Helmont. If she doesn't recognize him, then Helmont's out of the question. We might still go to the circus and try and succeed where Fournal failed and find someone else who really gave the ticket."

At the name of Fournal, Gallois made a gesture of amused contempt, and at that moment Travers caught sight of the photographer coming towards them across the road. He greeted Travers with particular friendliness and made no bones whatever about going back to the shop. When Travers told him in confidence that Helmont was certainly not a mysterious celebrity, he was perfectly willing to part with the photograph.

"So, for the first time I see this trapezist without a mask," announced Gallois, trying his English out on Lebrun. With much frowning he held the photograph to the light. "He is not without character, and he has good looks."

"Take it to the window, sir," Lebrun said. "You can see it better there."

But Gallois was all at once looking at nothing in particular, and mournfully shaking his head.

"Somewhere I have seen this man," he said, "and yet perhaps not. There is something which refuses to come back."

His lean fingers were feeling the air, and his brow was furrowed in the effort of thought.

"It is annoying when one is certain and yet cannot remember." In the light of the window he pored over the photograph, then handed it back with a gesture of resignation.

"Always it escapes," he said. "But about this photograph. It will be possible to prepare at once an enlargement?"

Lebrun said it should be ready first thing in the morning. Then he ventured on a question or two of his own. There was something fishy about the trapezist? Was that why he had rigged himself up in the mask?

The slang had left Gallois slightly puzzled, and it was Travers who made the non-committal replies and stressed the importance of absolute secrecy.

Then before dinner Gallois was ringing the authorities at Cannes and finding that the circus was leaving that night for Nice, where it would make a stay of two days. Then another idea came to him. He rang the Sûreté, and his lip had an ironic droop as he gave his brief report. There had been something after all, he said, in that anonymous communication from Toulon, and though, of course, it was incredible that Bariche could have survived the Auteuil fire, he considered it necessary to remain for a day or two to collect information which he hoped might prove not without interest.

Even at breakfast the following morning, Gallois had no idea what the day was to produce. The irony with which he had rung the Sûreté overnight was to recoil, as it were, upon himself. It was to be a dramatic irony, with himself as the unconscious victim.

But it was Charles who was really worrying him that early morning, and he was ready to admit that there was a certain irksomeness in his being out of things. So over the coffee he made his announcement. M. Travers and himself might have to be away that morning at the circus, and Charles might therefore do much worse than pay a visit to Lizou where Dr. Debran could remove the stitches. Charles found the prospect reasonably pleasing, but pointed out a difficulty. There was still the risk of hurting the feelings of both Dr. Debran and Gabrielle, who were doubtless imagining the party had been at Mariette and were now back in Paris. There was also the fact that in spite of having promised to write, not a single one of the three had ever sent a word.

"Explain," said Gallois ingratiatingly, "that M. Travers and myself were summoned to assist the law, since when we have not had a minute. Therefore you come to make our apologies and to announce that we return to Paris."

Charles made no more difficulties. Gallois discerned at once a rather too willing acquiescence.

"But this time you do not hire a car to go to Lizou," he said. "You will avail yourself of the *autobus*."

The two collected the photographs from the Rue des Alpes. The lens of the smaller camera must have been exceptionally good, for the enlargement was superb. Gallois was remarkably pleased, and then, as he nodded benignly, his expression was at once changing. He stared, then darted a quick look at Travers, but the eyes of Travers were elsewhere. Then Gallois was shaking his head, for he knew that what he had discovered—or had seemed to discern—was something utterly impossible. Then there was something else he was remembering—that stony track where Travers had met Helmont. Then once more he was shaking his head and preferring for the moment to regard the idea as fantastic.

"Something on your mind?" Travers was asking as they came out of the shop.

Gallois smiled dryly. "There is an anxiety, perhaps, about this Mme Dubois, and if she will recognize him. Always one is anxious when one holds in the hand a clue that may be of importance."

Mme Dubois was to prove the exactness of Aumade's description. Everything he had mentioned about her was easily enough discernible: the suspicious looks, the obvious wonder if there was some profit to be made, and behind everything the dull peasant sort of mind that is satisfied with its own powers and confident of the gullibility of others.

"You have seen this man before?" asked Gallois, showing the enlargement.

She did not know, she said, and was waiting to hear what was behind it all.

"This was not the man you saw behind the olive tree?"

She repeated, parrot fashion, what she had told Aumade, and how her eyes were none too good and the man had been a fair way off.

"Then was this the man who gave you the free ticket for the circus?"

She shook her head. That one had a moustache and wore glasses.

Gallois smiled with an immense patience. When at last he had induced her to describe the kind of moustache, he sketched it in on the original photograph and also added the glasses. As far as Mme Dubois was concerned he had wasted his time. What she was far more interested in was whether either of the gentlemen knew of a decent family who would care to employ her, now that the Villa Sablons was empty.

"There is one employer to whom I would offer her with satisfaction," Gallois said, as they walked back to the car. "And that is to the cousin of Mme Perthus. As for what she tells us about this Helmont, she is, as Aumade says, an imbecile. It is better, I think, that she should be ignored. For my part, I think this Helmont may have given the ticket and perhaps at Nice there will be something we discover for ourselves."

At the circus, Gallois decided to employ no artifices or circumlocutions. He did not exhibit his credentials, it is true, but there was an authority in the way he was asking for Pertini himself, and almost at once he and Travers were being shown into a handsome motor-caravan which served as the headquarters of the circus proprietor. Pertini was a little bright-eyed man with a skin that was very dark and a moustache that was snow white, and his manners were deferential to the point of obsequiousness.

"I did not wish to announce myself," Gallois said, putting the credentials back in his pocket, "because I prefer that this visit should be confidential. Publicity of the wrong kind is good neither for the person concerned not for the circus as a whole. Now I will ask you to be so good as to look at this photograph. Do you know who the person is?"

Pertini looked considerably surprised and admitted at once that it was M. Jules Helmont of the Helmont troupe of trapezists.

"It is possible to bring him here without attracting undue attention?" asked Gallois.

Pertini went to the door at once and called to someone to request M. Helmont to be so good as to come.

"There is nothing serious?" he asked Gallois in a state of much perturbation. "I cannot possibly imagine M. Helmont doing anything that would bring him into trouble with the law."

But Helmont was already mounting the steps. He cast the mildest of looks around him as he came in, though he could not conceal a quick surprise at the sight of Travers. Travers thought it as well to pretend something of surprise also. Gallois was already speaking.

"I am Gallois, Inspector of Police. You are Jules Helmont, the trapeze artist employed in this circus?"

"*A votre service, m'sieu l'inspecteur.*"

The voice was almost gentle, and nothing could have been more calm than his manner. He seemed politely surprised, though interested, when Gallois began describing briefly the murder of Letoque, but his eyes narrowed when it was announced that a witness had sworn that at the time of the murder a man of the exact description of himself had been seen in the neighbourhood of the Villa Sablons.

Gallois paused for an answer. Helmont looked blankly at Pertini, whose shrug of the shoulders was a gesture which indicated only too well that the witness who had stated such things was an utter fool. Helmont's lip drooped.

"It is absurd," he said. "It is absurd because it is impossible. At the time you mention I was miles from Carliens. I was in the mountains in my car."

Gallois smiled with almost a gratification.

"In order that this evidence which I have mentioned may be erased as incorrect, will you give the names of two witnesses who could prove you were not at Carliens?"

The gesture of Helmont announced that nothing would be more easy.

"Well?" said Gallois and waited.

Helmont grimaced. "Unfortunately, I know them but I do not know their names. If I saw them again I could easily recall myself to them."

There was a tap at the door and a man looked in. M. Helmont was wanted on the telephone at the box office.

"You will excuse me for a moment?" Helmont asked.

Gallois bowed charmingly and off Helmont went. Pertini was at once cutting in with questions, only to be deftly edged on one side. In the five minutes of Helmont's absence it was the circus itself in which Gallois was interested, and about which he had so many questions to ask.

"To resume then where we left off," Gallois said to Helmont. "You are absolutely sure you will be able to furnish me with the witnesses I request?"

"Absolutely certain," Helmont told him.

Gallois smiled with enormous satisfaction.

"That will be admirable. All that remains to do is to inspect your papers."

"That unfortunately is impossible," Helmont said regretfully. "My papers have been either lost or stolen."

Gallois surveyed him with mournful, sympathetic eyes.

"That is unfortunate, as you say. You reported the loss to the necessary authorities?"

Helmont made a gesture of even greater regret.

"But you know how it is. At every moment I've been expecting the papers to turn up again, and so it got put off and put off. All the same, I'm prepared to answer any questions whatever which you care to put to me."

Gallois with an extreme deliberation wrote in his note-book that Jules Nevers, professional name Helmont, aged thirty-four, had been born at Lille of French parents, and then to the enormous surprise of Travers he was stating that the interview was at an end. There did follow a warning, however. In the morning Helmont must be prepared to accompany the police to interview those witnesses whom he had promised to secure. In the meantime, Gallois reminded him that the arm of the law was very long. A word of thanks to Pertini and he was making his way down the caravan steps.

"That story of his seems remarkably unconvincing to me," said Travers as soon as they were out of earshot. "Are you sure he won't try to get away?"

Gallois smiled with a confidence that was almost complacent, but Travers was still far from being convinced. The methods of Gallois, though doubtless not without purpose, seemed for once careless to the point of danger.

"And that story about his papers. Didn't that seem a bit extraordinary to you?"

"If he produces the witnesses, then the papers are unnecessary," Gallois said. "You and I are not clerks and officials who make miserable the lives of people with their documents. We desire the assassin of Letoque, not papers of identification."

Just short of the exit he paused for a moment and took a quick look round.

"And now, my friend, there is something it is necessary to do. Discover at the telephone bureau where this call comes from that arrives just now for M. Helmont. In ten minutes I join you there, and then perhaps there are things which may happen."

CHAPTER XV
THE ANTICLIMAX

ONE THING Travers had not mentioned to Gallois. He also, now he had seen Helmont again in the flesh, was convinced that somewhere or other he had run up against him in some place far removed from the cross-roads on that Monday afternoon of the murder of Rionne. Indeed he might have been worrying his wits in an effort to solve that minor mystery had not the major mystery of the queer conduct of Gallois superimposed itself.

For the conduct of Gallois in that brief inquiry had certainly been inexplicable. Never had an interrogation been more mild and informal. It had been, in fact, like a fond parent reluctantly reprimanding a delinquent son. No cross-examination, no threats of confrontation with Mme Dubois, no demanding an alibi for that vital time when the circus ticket had actually been given—nothing, in fact, but a calm and almost grateful acceptance of each lame and unsupported statement.

And then Travers paused in the act of pushing the starter of his car, and his fingers went to his glasses instead. There were those last words of Gallois that things were shortly about to happen. His conduct, then, had been premeditated guile, and he was contemplating some *coup*. Then what was the new information he had secured and the facts he had deduced? Travers shook his head. Something there certainly was, and it was something which Gallois obviously thought Travers had seen for himself, and as he drove slowly back to town, Travers was puzzling his wits to find what that something was and achieving nothing at all.

Perhaps he might have been even more puzzled if he had been with Gallois at that moment. It was to the box office of the circus which was outside the main entrance that Gallois made his way. He noted the telephone wire, undoubtedly rigged up by local engineers so that patrons in the town could book their seats. The woman who sat in the bureau informed him that such arrangements were made at every town of consequence.

"This M. Helmont is a man of a suspicious mind," Gallois remarked with his sad romantic smile.

She gave a quick interrogative look.

"When he was speaking on the telephone just now didn't he ask you to go out for a moment or two?"

"You saw him then?" she said.

Gallois smiled apologetically. "I am naturally a curious individual," he said. "Not that it matters about M. Helmont, and I don't really know why I mentioned it. Perhaps it was because I wished to continue speaking to yourself."

A minute or two and he was making his leisurely way to the road. Once out of sight of the bureau he strode on at speed. Then he was lucky enough to find a taxi and in a couple of minutes was at the main post office. From there he rang the Sûreté, and when at last he arrived at telephone headquarters Travers had been waiting for some minutes. He also had news. The telephone message had come from Gevrol.

Gallois seemed pleased, yet disappointed.

"Then the story of this Helmont agrees," he said. "There are mountains at Gevrol, and there, at a café perhaps, or a garage, he doubtless sees those who are to be witnesses for his alibi. Also it was on the way to Gevrol that, you saw him that Monday afternoon."

"And what do we do now?" asked Travers and felt as if the bottom had rather fallen out of things.

"Now we return to Carliens," Gallois said. "We do not wish a second accident or stitches in the skull like those of Charles, but it seems to me that we should go to Carliens with speed. For my part, I shall not distract your attention with words, and I have what you call the nerve. Drive fast then, my friend."

So Gallois withdrew into his thoughts. Travers concentrated on the car, and while he took no chances he drove as fast as he had ever driven. Just short of Carliens, Gallois was asking for the car to be slowed up.

"Perhaps it would be best if we do not go direct to Gevrol," he said. "First we go to the hotel where perhaps you will have the goodness to obtain quickly a cold meal and a bottle which we will take with us. And request the confidence of M. Velot that Charles is not informed. For me, it will be necessary to borrow, if possible, from M. Velot a pair of glasses."

Charles was back from Lizou and having lunch, and while Velot was cleaning the field-glasses Gallois had a word with him. The stitches had been removed, but he thought both the doctor and Gabrielle had been hurt at the news that the three had been so near all the time, and yet had never even troubled to telephone.

"Then you did not make our excuses, as I asked," said Gallois annoyedly.

"But I did," Charles told him. "I told them all about the murder and how M. Aumade insisted on your help. I said you would have accompanied me this morning, if you had not had to go to Nice on the same business."

"There was no necessity to tell the whole world about the inquiries," Gallois said, with what Charles rightly considered an unreasonableness. "It isn't a topic that one discusses with friends."

"But why shouldn't I discuss it?" demanded Charles, hands already vibrating impatiently. "Even if you do not know it yourself, I assure you that the Debrans are people of discretion and they are my friends, and as a matter of fact they were very interested in everything."

Never had the smile of Gallois been so tender and disarming. His hand fell and gently patted the head of Charles.

"*Pardon.* It is you who are right and I who am wrong. Now I will leave you to get on with your lunch. M. Travers and I have one little matter of business to conclude."

"You're going to the Hôtel de Ville?" Charles asked. "M. Aumade seemed to think it was rather urgent."

Travers, already waiting at the car, explained that allusion to the Hôtel de Ville and Aumade, for Velot had told him that Fournal had been round twice that morning with an urgent message. Apparently there had been new developments. But Gallois was dismissing Aumade with a gesture of indifference, and no sooner was he in the car than he was once more requesting speed. As the Rolls climbed steadily up from the town he began to explain. Helmont would be off to Gevrol to find those witnesses, but it was just as well to be there before him and keep him under observation. If an alibi was in the process of being manufactured then in the morning Helmont would receive a very great surprise.

As far as Gallois was concerned there was one annoying episode as they drew near Lizou. Three cows suddenly emerged from the road that turned from Cannes into their own road and the car had to pull up dead. The road was narrow and the man who drove the cows was either deaf or obstinate, for he made little effort to keep the animals to one side, and it was only with difficulty that at last the car edged through. Gallois was looking impatiently back for fear that Helmont's car should come into sight.

"Well," said Travers cheerfully when at last they were through, "there is one consolation. If Helmont is close behind us, those cows are going to hold him up now, so that we haven't really lost anything." Then he was chuckling. "Charles would have been amused; he seems to have a perfect horror of animals nowadays. We passed a couple of cows on the road to Cannes the other day and he said he'd never hear a cow moo again without thinking he was still in bed and his cars buzzing."

"Slowly now, if you please," Gallois was saying. "It might perhaps be better if we did not go all the way to Gevrol."

Just as they were entering the tiny town, his hand went out and he was indicating a narrow lane that ran down to a little farm. Travers drew the car in and reversed in order to be able to move off again at once. The farmer appeared and Gallois asked permission for the car to remain there for a few minutes. Then, carrying the lunch, he set off down the meadow that fell steeply to the valley bottom. Then he turned right till the little stream narrowed and he could jump across. There was a straggly grove of olives that made shelter and shade and when he had climbed for a minute or two he looked across the valley through his glasses, then passed them to Travers and suggested lunch.

From where they sat, as Travers could see, the road out of Lizou was plainly visible, bends and all, and there was something he thought he recognized. Gallois had another look through the glasses and confirmed that it was the house of the Debrans. Just along to the left was the little cottage of the *cantonnier*, and through the glasses one could see the very gap in the brick wall through which Charles's car had toppled after the accident.

The two began their lunch with an eye always on the road. Travers knew that Gallois must have stayed behind that morning at the circus to familiarize himself with the car that Helmont would use, for when a car did pass from the direction of Lizou, a quick look through the glasses was enough to satisfy him that their own man had not yet appeared. Lunch was over, a cigarette had been smoked and then another, and it was after two o'clock when something happened.

Travers had been daydreaming for a moment, but was suddenly aware that Gallois was looking through the glasses across the valley. He seemed to have seen something himself, and then he knew he had been deceived, for when he looked along the road towards Gevrol there was never a car moving. But Gallois must have seen something unusual, for he was getting to his feet.

"You've seen him?" Travers said.

"I think so."

With no more words he was making his way down from the olives. The little stream was crossed again and then he was not making for the farm and the car, but straight across the valley. From the bottom the road had been hidden, and as they drew near to the opposite slope he was motioning Travers back and crawling up on hands and knees and taking a precautionary peep. Then still keeping out of sight of the road, he moved on some distance to the right, and when at last they came through the broken-down wall they were half-way between the doctor's house and the scene of Charles's accident.

With never a word Gallois turned towards the village. Just short of the wall that formed the boundary for the garden of the doctor's house, he halted and motioned for Travers to look.

"There's a car there," Travers said. "It's Helmont's car! What on earth's he doing there?"

Gallois frowned and his own voice lowered.

"That is something I also wish to discover," he said. "You, my friend, remain here and observe the car. If Helmont appears, then you call loudly to him and you stop him. If he escapes without the car then you follow and you call all the time to attract help."

At once he was moving on. His feet made no sound on the grass, and he was keeping to the screening shelter of the trees. Travers, peering cautiously round, saw him make a quick movement towards the door and heard the sound of his knock.

Ten minutes went by, and Travers's heart, which had been beating so violently, was now almost normal. Then all at once Gallois appeared and was calling to him from the porch. Travers went down the path and it seemed that Gallois himself was in charge of the house, for there was no one else at the door.

"Come in," Gallois said. "There are explanations which are delayed until you arrive."

He led the way into the dining-room. The doctor was there and Gabrielle, and seated apart in an attitude of some dejection was Helmont. It was at Gabrielle that Travers ventured first to look and it was her eyes that fell.

"M. Travers and I have been wrong," Gallois said. "But as I explained to you it was not altogether our own fault. When you are the servants of the law, as we are, you have to obey orders, and if your brother persists in acting as though he has something to conceal, he mustn't grumble if he throws suspicion on himself."

Travers already knew. Until that day at the fork he had never clapped eyes on Helmont, but he had seen Gabrielle and she had remained as a near and most charming memory, and now between the brother and the sister he was seeing again the overwhelming likeness.

"My apologies," Travers said lamely. "I feel I have repaid very badly all your kindnesses."

"No, no!" Debran said hastily. "As M. Gallois has said, the fault is entirely our own."

"Nevertheless," said Gallois, "there is one matter in which I do most earnestly ask for the corroboration of M. Travers. He will assure you, as I did, that Charles arrived here this morning with no thought but friendliness and gratitude. He, at the moment, is not concerned with the police. It was not till we actually saw your brother this morning that we noticed the remarkable likeness to yourselves. Then your brother said he had been with friends near Gevrol and M. Travers recalled that he had seen your brother one afternoon in his car and he had asked the way to Lizou. That is why we came here to inquire, and the first thing we saw was your brother's car, which M. Travers recognized."

"I assure you there is no need for apologies," the doctor said. "As for Charles, it is impossible that he should ever act with duplicity. We always knew he came here this morning in good faith. And now will you permit me to explain?"

The story was simple and lucid. Jules Debran was a gymnast of superb agility with a post at the army training-school at Nancy. Then he received an offer from someone who wished to turn his talents to account, and the offer was so lucrative that he abandoned his army career and formed the Helmont Troupe. This his family naturally considered a disgrace. Their father had been an army surgeon of considerable repute—Gallois himself had heard of him and knew at least one of his books—and Jules was warned that if he persisted in adopting the new career he would cease to be a member of his family.

Then the Grand Cirque Pertini arrived at Carliens, and Jules at once had a kind of homesickness and a longing to see Gabrielle. He did see her on that Monday afternoon when Rionne was stabbed and he found her alone. But the doctor came back unexpectedly from Gevrol and caught him there. There was a scene, but thanks to Gabrielle it ended in reconciliation. As soon as the present contract expired Jules was abandoning his career, but during the short stay of the circus at Carliens he left his work to his understudy and saw as much of his brother and sister as possible. The reason why he had lied that morning was that the main thing he wished was for it not to be known that the brother of Dr. Debran and Gabrielle was a performer in a circus.

Then that morning, Charles, in that very room, had told the doctor and Gabrielle, in all good faith and in strict confidence, about the inquiries Gallois and Travers were making. And he had chanced to add that a trapezist at the circus was under suspicion.

"Jules had told us how we could always get in touch with him," Debran said, "so at once we rang him up."

"It was I who rang," Gabrielle said. "I went specially to Gertol so that Jules should not think we were incriminating him in any way. I implored him to tell us what it was he had been doing and to explain. He assured me that he had done nothing, but I made him promise to come here at once."

"It is I who have caused all this disturbance and worry," Jules said humbly. "As for the alibi about which you were inquiring this morning, it must have been someone who was either blind or mad who said I was seen in Carliens that Wednesday afternoon."

"He was here, as we have told you," Gabrielle said.

"It is of no consequence," began Gallois. "I assure you—"

"Even Charles himself knew he was here," Debran said.

"I do not know," Jules pointed out. "I saw him, but he didn't see me. Gabrielle called to me when he awoke, because she thought you were asleep and she didn't want to disturb you, but you woke and told me to stay where I was. You remember, when you were putting on your dressing-gown just before you went in."

As Travers and Gallois returned to Carliens each was uneasy and somehow ashamed. It was not because a mistake had been made, as Gallois said, for the very mistake had arisen out of a series of acute deductions of which he was very far from being ashamed. But what the two could not rid themselves of was the feeling that there had been left in the house of the Debrans something of under-handedness. Kindness and hospitality had been ill repaid and in spite of all protestations to the contrary, there had been a difference and even something of pain in the eyes of both Gabrielle and the doctor. All the old warmth of feeling had been swept away in one unlucky moment; something fine had been tarnished and could never be the same again. From Debran and Gabrielle there might be a welcome—innate courtesy would ensure that—and yet both Gallois and Travers knew that never could they set foot in Lizou again.

At the hotel Velot had a message. Once more M. Aumade had sent word that he would be grateful for the presence of Gallois and Travers. Ten minutes later, the two were on their way to the Hôtel de Ville.

CHAPTER XVI
AUMADE CONCLUDES

WHAT AUMADE HAD to say was promising enough for a final solution of the mystery. Unknown to any one, a man had been searching the vicinity of the Villa Sablons and at last he had discovered the gun. It had been rushed to Toulon, and tests had proved it was the same gun that had been used by the murderer of Letoque. When he escaped through the back of the house, the murderer had undoubtedly hidden it under the pine needles at the foot of the tree, where it had been found. It was a Mark 27—short barrel—issue of which had ceased in 1926.

"Colonel Brassier might possibly have been issued with such a revolver," Aumade said, and there was something questioning in his tone.

"He owned a revolver?" asked Gallois.

"Ah!" said Aumade, and pounced on the question at once. "Listen to what happened. I decided to act warily and invited the Colonel here for an informal talk on revolvers, and in the meanwhile I arranged that Mme Brassier should be interrogated at her house. She admitted there had been an affair with Letoque and his passion had cooled, and that Wednesday afternoon she had determined to see him. She knew where her husband's revolver was kept, but when she went to get it, it was gone. What she had wanted it for was not to shoot Letoque. What she was going to do was to threaten suicide in his presence; to induce him in fact to begin the affair all over again! But, as she said, the revolver was not there, though that was not the reason why she kept in her own garden, and went no farther than the gap in the hedge. This was the reason: *From the glasses she saw that her husband was not with his daughter on the beach.*"

The eyes of Gallois narrowed.

"Yes," he said. "And she knew of his jealousy."

"Undoubtedly," said Aumade. "But wait a minute. We did not interrogate the daughter for fear of arousing too much suspicion, but Mine Brassier said she had questioned her carefully herself as soon as she suspected it was her husband who had done the murder. She even accused her husband of the murder and he swore he had been all the time on the beach with Lucille.

"But as she triumphantly and doubtless venomously assured him, Lucille had already admitted that no sooner had she arrived with her father on the beach than he was saying that there was something he had forgotten and she might sunbathe perhaps till he came back. In fact," said Aumade, "my opinion is that Mme Brassier has him absolutely in her clutches and was threatening she would come to us and tell all she knew."

"And what did Brassier say?" asked Travers.

"Ah!" said Aumade. "I lengthened out this informal talk I was having about revolvers, in the course of which, by the way, the Colonel admitted he had a revolver himself though it had been lost for some weeks. He suspected a theft by some workmen who had been in the house. Then as soon as word came through to me here of the information that had just been obtained from his wife, I changed my tone."

He paused to give a smile of a man who has pulled off an exceedingly lucky deal.

"Naturally I requested explanations. His statements were too conflicting to be reconciled. Mind you, I did not mention the source of my information and I also admit that I tried a bluff. I said I could prove he was not on the beach, and furthermore that he had been seen in the vicinity of the Villa Sablons just before the shots. I requested an immediate confession."

He was shaking his head and the story was left like that, in the air.

"But the good Colonel decided to say nothing?" asked Gallois dryly.

"Admitted. He took refuge in silence. I said to him, 'Colonel Brassier, you are a man of honour and you prefer to say nothing which would damage the good name of yourself and your family. Very well then, go back to your house, but be prepared at any moment to be recalled here and to admit the truth. If not, I shall have no compunction whatever in ordering your immediate arrest, which will call down on your head the very scandal you wish to avoid.' Then he went and naturally I took steps to keep his house under close observation."

"And now you are about to interrogate him in earnest," said Gallois.

"Precisely," said Aumade, and was making for the desk, but as his fingers went out there was the sound of the buzzer. He took up the receiver and his eyes were goggling at once.

"Mon dieu—non!"

Against the background of the blurred voice that spoke, there were grunting from Aumade and quick gestures of impatience. A moment and the receiver was thrust back in place. Aumade got to his feet and there was tragedy in his tone.

"Gentlemen, the affair is over. This Brassier has shot himself!"

A superb dramatic gesture and then without comment he was making for the door. The two must have been supposed to follow, for he stopped abruptly and ushered them through. A car was waiting and the three got in. Not a word was said till the Villa Sablons was neared, for Gallois had no wish to intrude on the disappointment and chagrin of Aumade. Then it was Aumade himself who spoke.

"It was not Fournal but myself who was the fool," he said. "I wished to be clever and finish everything at once, and now see what has happened."

The car was stopping and Fournal himself was waiting outside the Villa Sablons. With no more than a salute he led the way round to the back and up the rough steps to the path behind, and beyond it to the wood. Fifty yards up the slope there was an old stone wall, and by it lay the body of Brassier, a gun in his hand.

"And now, what happened?" demanded Aumade.

Fournal said that according to instructions he and his two men had watched the house, both back and front. There had been the sound of violent voices and half an hour previously Mme Brassier had left the house by the front gate carrying a small bag, as if she were going away. Fournal sent one of his men to follow her, but she went no farther than the Hôtel Mirande where she was at that moment. Shortly afterwards

Colonel Brassier suddenly appeared at the back of the house and Fournal kept him under observation. He strode up and down like a man in the depth of despair, then all at once was striding away up the slope.

"What I thought," said Fournal, "was that he was not aware that we had removed the gun and was going to get it, but he didn't go that way at all. He went this way and before I could get here there was a sound of a shot and—*voilà!*"

"He knew the gun had been removed," Aumade said exasperatedly. "He must have deduced the fact to-day, even if he didn't find out days ago."

"Then he had two guns," said Fournal.

"You make your deductions too late," Aumade told him bitterly. "Obviously he had two guns and with this one he shot himself. But it was his wife who killed him. Even if he had not been guilty of the death of Letoque, her evidence would have been enough. She would have told any lies to send him to the guillotine, and he knew it."

There followed a quick reconstruction of the events of that fatal Wednesday afternoon. Brassier had guessed from his wife's manner that she was intending to visit Letoque, and he planned accordingly. He intended to enter the Villa Sablons and confront the guilty pair, but he found Letoque alone. There was a brief but violent scene. Brassier threatened Letoque with the gun and Letoque was killed. Out went Brassier by the back way and his wife just caught a glimpse of him. He paused only to conceal the gun, then made a rapid way back to the beach where doubtless he exhibited to his daughter whatever it was he had been to fetch.

The *affaire Letoque* was over. The thanks of M. Aumade had been uttered once more, the compliments exchanged and the farewells said. Travers and Gallois were making a slow way back to the hotel.

"What is it that amuses you?" Gallois asked suddenly, and he was looking somewhat amused himself.

"The whole thing is so grotesque", Travers told him. "It is absurd the case ending like this. You're surely not satisfied, are you?"

"On the contrary," Gallois told him blandly. "I am satisfied and M. Aumade is satisfied and the whole world will be satisfied. M. Aumade returns with a good conscience to his vines from which he tore himself with much difficulty, and I return to Paris with the dossier of Bariche, which, by the morning, will be completed."

Travers smiled "Splendid. The only person who isn't satisfied seems to be me. But honestly, *mon ami*, and strictly between ourselves, aren't there also a lot of things that are not so satisfying? By the wall was lying a stone that came out of the hole where Brassier had hidden the gun with which he shot himself. He didn't know anything about the other gun, but went to get the one he had hidden there and he shot himself because he thought his wife had given the actual one that did the killing to the police, and he knew he'd never prove it wasn't he who had shot Letoque."

"Brassier was an imbecile," Gallois said. "It was the brains of his wife he should have blown out and not his own."

"Maybe," said Travers. "But I am absolutely positive he didn't kill Letoque."

"Gently, my friend," said Gallois with a humorous reproof. "What a tragedy if a promenader should overhear and repeat to our good Aumade something that might even keep him from his vines." His face straightened somewhat. "And you think that that afternoon Brassier knew Letoque was dead?"

Again Travers was smiling. "I think precisely the same as you do. Brassier had heard the sounds and he went to investigate and found Letoque dead. At once he hid his own gun in the stone wall and was making for the beach again as hard as he could go."

"But if Brassier was not the murderer, why did he not see the real murderer depart?"

"Perhaps he did, from a distance," Travers said. "And he thought it was Mme Brassier. Perhaps therefore he did not actually hear the shots, but only saw someone leave the villa, and he took that someone for his wife. At once he went in to confront Letoque and found him dead."

Then it was Gallois who was smiling. "My friend, let us not concern ourselves with these problems. They are, as I say, for the excellent Aumade."

They were passing a café and he was taking Travers by the arm and directing him to a chair.

"You and I," he said, "will drink to the termination of this affair. By the morning I shall possess some more information for the convincing of certain people that the *affaire* of Auteuil was not all that they regarded it. We drink also to M. Aumade, who will never know that he has occupied himself not with the *affaire Letoque*, but the *affaire Bariche*. For the last thing these certain gentlemen in Paris will do is to acknowledge to the world that they were wrong. And we will drink to ourselves, also, for to-morrow at this time I shall be in the train for Paris."

"But we shall be meeting again there later," Travers reminded him.

He drank the toast nevertheless and then Gallois was saying something which he did rather hope to hear.

"There is perhaps a regret that the affair does not end itself with a perfection, even though it is not the concern of ourselves to announce the things which M. Aumade fails to observe. There is, for example, the problem of that man who gave to Mme Dubois the circus ticket." His lip drooped. "But doubtless if we mention the matter to our good Aumade, he will prefer to regard this giver of free tickets as an agent of Colonel Brassier, employed to ensure that Mme Brassier should compromise herself at the right moment."

"Yes," said Travers. "But the really difficult problem to my mind is still this, X gave Mme Dubois the circus ticket to get her out of the house. X was not Brassier, that's certain, though Aumade might claim that he was employed by Brassier as part of a trap to catch his wife *in flagrante delicto* but the fact remains that Letoque himself made all this superfluous by giving Mme Dubois a holiday, and that not to see Mme Perthus, because he hadn't the faintest idea where she was. Nor was it to see Mme

Brassier, because he had no plans arranged with her and that particular passion had cooled off. Then who was Letoque expecting at the Villa Sablons? Was it X or was it some person we have never even heard of?"

Gallois leaned across the table and patted him on the shoulder.

"My friend, if it had been you and I in charge of this affair we should not have been satisfied with a solution so facile and which arrives at so fortunate a moment for our friend Aumade. Nevertheless I am at your service. If you insist, we remain here a day or two, unknown to Aumade, and we will try to find the answer to the questions which you have so admirably put,"

"Heavens, no!" said Travers. "I'm not prepared to be that kind of a nuisance, and I do see your point of view. You've achieved an ambition and I'm twenty times more pleased about it than if it was something I'd done myself." He shook his head. "No. The fact is I have a far too tidy mind that hates loose ends and—well, that's sometimes my misfortune."

"But no," protested Gallois. "It is this tidy mind than makes you the superb artist that you are."

Travers smiled.

"Nonsense, my dear fellow, nonsense. But I also should tell you that I have some very undetective-like prejudices. I am quite satisfied to call the case over, and for this reason. You remember the little argument with Charles the other day? I didn't support him against you, but I'll own up to you now that I was very much on his side. I'd hate to see any one guillotined for the sake of Bariche. Whoever killed him did something that was very long overdue."

Gallois smiled a grave reproof.

"Among friends it is always good that there should be confidences, and I also will make a confession. For me there is the shame that here in my heart I know that this Brassier is not the assassin of Bariche. It is necessary that to-morrow I go to Paris. Nevertheless, even now, if there comes to me an idea which seems to arrive at this assassin, I am Gallois and I remain."

He was getting to his feet and his mournful eyes had in them an enormous affection.

"You forgive, perhaps, what I say? There are all types, as one says, that make a world. You, my friend, are this and I am that. But it is enough that together as collaborators there is nothing which we cannot achieve. And now we go to find this Charles, who to-morrow also returns to Paris."

After dinner Gallois went up to his room and wrote his notes. Travers stayed with him for a few minutes and while he was there Gallois was called to the telephone. When he came back he handed to Travers, with quite a carelessness, the report that had just come in from the Sûreté, and explained how he had come to receive it.

"At Nice this morning, when I was sure that Helmont was Debran, I telephoned to Paris and requested this information, which now arrives. Now it is of no importance except to tell us again what we already know."

He was settling to his notes once more and Travers went down to find Charles. Velot said that M. Rabaud had gone out for a walk in the cool evening, and so in the lounge Travers read the report on the Debran family, that had come from Paris.

As Gallois had said, it gave no new information. It began at the father, Robert Hippolyte Debran, the famous surgeon and author. His wife, Henriette Paulet, a member of the wealthy Paulet family of Tours, had outlived her husband and had died, in fact, that last winter. The sons were Gaston, believed to be in Indo-China; Robert, army surgeon, retired; and Jules, officer in the gymnastic corps, also retired. The daughters were Gabrielle, nurse, in the hospital of St. Claire, Montmartre, now retired; and Denise, wife of the late Henri Lannes of Dijon, now married again and believed to be abroad.

Charles came in then. It had been colder than he thought outside, and he was deciding to stay indoors instead. Then he invited Travers to play billiards, and ten o'clock came before they were aware of it. When Travers went up, he peeped into Gallois's room, but he was not there.

And so to the final morning of that curious, unexpected and somehow dramatic holiday that Travers had spent in Carliens. Gallois literally gulped down his coffee and said he had a hundred things to do but he would be back in ample time for the train.

"What did he mean by train?" Travers asked Charles. "Surely I'm driving you both to Marseilles and you can catch the express there?"

Charles shrugged his shoulders. "This morning he has a what you call—" He abandoned his English. "He has something on his mind. When he gets these queer fits I can always tell. He boasts sometimes that he can read me like a book, but it is I who can read him as easily as I read that advertisement on the wall."

"I expect he's anxious to get all his notes from M. Aumade," Travers said.

"Perhaps," said Charles. "All the same there is no reason why he should hurry back like this to Paris. When he told me this morning he would catch the ten o'clock train here and go to Marseilles to connect with the express, I told him that in your car we should arrive just as soon, and it would be much more pleasant. But for once he didn't wish to argue, and that again is a sign that he's got something on his mind."

Travers smiled. "Perhaps you're right. All the same I think it's just natural anxiety. What you'd expect on the last morning after a holiday."

"But it was last night too," Charles said. "What do you think he did? Came into my room and woke me up after midnight. Wanted to know if that newspaper I'd seen at Lizou on the Wednesday afternoon had had anything in it about Rionne's murder."

"Why not?" asked Travers amusedly. "Mightn't that have been something to do with the notes he was writing. Perhaps he wanted some verification or other."

At half-past nine Gallois was back again, and as they sat for a last yarn before it was time for Travers to take them to the station, Travers himself was aware in half a dozen ways that Gallois did indeed have something on his mind, and he knew it not so much by what Gallois let fall as by what he was so obviously endeavouring to conceal. Then the time came. The car moved off and old Velot was waving farewells from the hotel door. Out came the luggage at the station and Gallois had a last request to make.

"Discover if you will, my friend," he said to Travers, "the exact hour at which the train arrives at Marseilles. You will find the announcement on the platform."

But Travers found a porter just through the door to the platform and had the information at once. Charles was busy elsewhere with another porter and the luggage, while Gallois was obtaining the tickets, and as Travers came up behind the back of Gallois, who was unaware of him, Travers heard something extraordinarily strange. Gallois was asking for two tickets, and not to Paris. One ticket was to Marseilles, *and the other to Furolles*.

Travers moved quietly off again and at once was trying to think, but in a moment Gallois was with him and then Charles, and in a minute or two every one was on the move, for the train was coming in. Another two minutes and it was going out again, and Travers waved till it had disappeared round the bend, and with it the mournful face of Gallois and the waving handkerchief of Charles.

Our by the car, Travers again was trying desperately to think. Why should Gallois be going to Furolles? And then suddenly he thought he know. An idea *had* come to Gallois—the idea of which he had spoken—the idea which would lead him to the assassin of Bariche. But who was there at Furolles who could have killed Bariche? Only Cippe, and he bore no resemblance whatever to the man who had given the circus ticket to Mme Dubois.

Travers shook his head, got into the car and slowly drove into the station yard. Then the car was held up. Just ahead of him were half a dozen sheep being driven into the yard of a local butcher, and as the drover herded them into the narrow way they were bleating noisily. But the road was clear again and Travers went on.

Then suddenly be was bringing the car to a halt. That he was almost on the crown of the road he was wholly unaware, for his horn-rims were in his hand and he was slowly polishing them.

Then all at once he was giving a gasp, of which even Aumade might have been proud, and as one hand replaced the glasses the other moved forward the lever and the car shot on again.

But it did not stop at the hotel. With increasing speed it went on, turned round by the car park, shot by the hotel again, then turned sharp right past the Villa Vézac, and was making for Lizou at a speed that was almost terrifying.

CHAPTER XVII
GALLOIS ARRIVES

As HE NEARED Lizou, Travers was slowly recognizing the fact that he was like a man driving headlong into dangerous unknown country with never a map to guide him. At the end of that journey there would be things to say, and at the moment he had scarcely a word prepared. All that was driving him was instinct, and a few suspicions.

So he stopped the car and found a piece of rough paper on which to write down his thoughts. To arrive with nothing but surmise would be madness, and yet, now he came to get down to hard facts, there was little that he really knew. If only he could ring up Charles! One minute's talk and everything might be clear. But Gallois had taken care of that. He had sent Charles to Marseilles, out of the way of talk, and after having obtained those vital facts for which Travers would have given an enormous deal.

"Yes," said Travers to himself. "Gallois knows. Last night he pretended to be indifferent, but those words must have struck him as they struck me—only the disaster of it is that they didn't really strike me till I remembered them this morning."

He was shaking his head and spreading his palms in a Gallic gesture of helplessness, and then out of the very helplessness something arrived.

"Wait a minute," said Travers to himself. "Gallois knows, and he's perfectly sure that I don't know. Very well then. If Gallois knows, and he's made preparations unknown to me—as he thinks—to make an arrest, then I also must be right! What are suspicious to me are facts to him. Very well then, I'll assume here and now that all my suspicions are absolute facts."

He was nodding to himself at that comforting determination, and then was thinking of something else. Himself and Charles in an argument against Gallois. Two claiming—perhaps none too seriously—that the killer of Bariche did not deserve the guillotine, but Gallois taking himself seriously enough and—if the expediency of getting back to Paris need not be sacrificed—determined to bring the killer to justice, whoever that killer was. Gallois, even as late as at dinner the previous night, had never expected to receive even a hint of that killer, and yet that hint had miraculously come, and out of it he had built a case.

"Yes," said Travers. "It arrived when I was with Charles last night, and after that he avoided me. He wasn't in his bedroom, and perhaps he was out even then making fresh inquiries. This morning Charles knew he had something on his mind. Now both of us—the scrupulous ones, as Gallois thinks us—have been side-tracked. Charles is on the way to Marseilles without knowing a thing, and Gallois thinks I'm spending another day or two in Carliens before going on to Marseilles to meet Bernice."

But all that was very well. The vital thing at that moment was, just what clinching proof was it that Gallois had discovered which he—Travers—did not possess. And then Travers suddenly had an idea. Gallois might be congratulating himself that he had sequestrated, as it were, two exceedingly awkward and far too scrupulous and tender-hearted allies, but there was someone he had not sequestrated. And at once Travers was moving the car on. If he had driven fast before, he now drove recklessly on his tyres and brakes.

As he neared Gevrol he slowed, and it was almost decorously that he drew up before the door of Dr. Favre, and with a relief that in front of it there had been standing no other car. At once he was being shown into the dining-room where the old doctor had been sitting over his newspaper. He was most surprised to see Travers who, he had imagined, was back in England days ago.

Travers explained that he was indeed just on the way to Marseilles, but had come the few miles out of his way to correct an error. The M. Charles Rabaud whom Dr. Favre had attended at Lizou, was still in the doctor's debt, and he—Travers—had come to pay the balance. On Dr. Favre's bill were two visits, but there ought to have been three: one on the Tuesday morning, one on the Tuesday evening, and one on the Wednesday evening,

"But, no," Favre said, "There was the one visit on the Tuesday, It was from about six o'clock till—well, perhaps a quarter past." Then his eyes were opening wide. "And you have come all this way to correct a mistake which did not exist!"

"So it seems," said Travers ruefully. "All the same, it gives me the opportunity, on behalf of M. Rabaud, to thank you for all you did for him, and to say a personal good-bye to you myself."

The doctor was highly gratified, though claiming that Debran and Gabrielle had done everything. Still in his carpet slippers he came shambling out with Travers to the door, and his farewells had a warmth of which Travers would never have suspected him.

But in spite of that one damning fact that he had discovered, Travers, as he drove back, was smiling somewhat ruefully again. Now he had definitely committed himself, and there might be the devil to pay. And yet, he could tell himself, old Favre was not the excitable kind. Age had made him slipshod, and it was odds against his taking the trouble to telephone, In any case the risk would have to be run, and at once he was ordering his thoughts in the light of the new evidence. By the time he was back in Lizou he had something of a case prepared.

He drove the car into the little garage and asked if it might stay there an hour or two out of the sun. And it was on foot that he made his way to the doctor's house. There was no concealment, and it was openly that he walked down the path. Then, before his hand could go out to the bell, the door opened. Gabrielle must have heard steps and looked out, for she was all at once there. She was smiling, but it was in her eyes that he saw the watchfulness, and perhaps even a fright.

"*Bonjour*, Gabrielle." Never had he tried to make a smile more friendly. "I've come to say a really last good-bye. The doctor is in?"

"No," she said. "He is visiting a patient in the mountains."

"But mayn't I come in?"

She let out a breath that might have been of relief.

"Of course. How stupid of me. And you are leaving at once then for Marseilles?"

"Almost at once," he said, and his tone was deliberately grave.

She stopped there, at the *salon* door.

"Something has happened? To M. Charles?"

"No," he said. "Every one is well, and yet—well, something has happened. Something I want to talk about."

"To me?"

"Yes," he said gravely. "To you."

Now she was really alarmed.

"But I don't understand—"

"Sit down, won't you?" he said. "And I'll sit here, where I can see through the window." He smiled as he shook his head. "You see, nobody knows I've come here, M. Charles is already on his way back to Paris, but M. Gallois pretended to be going to Paris, whereas he went only to Furolles. In a very few minutes, perhaps, he will be arriving here. I came first, because I wanted to talk to you, and warn you."

"But I don't understand." She was making a brave show of it, with her smile and her gesture of bewilderment. "Why should M. Gallois be coming here?"

He shook his head again.

"Monsieur Gallois is not coming here. It is *Inspector* Gallois who is coming here. Now do you not understand?"

There was still something heroic in the shake of the head, but there was tragedy in her eyes. The fingers that had been so placid on her lap were fidgeting nervously. Travers leaned forward, and his voice had an earnestness that had in it something of pain.

"Gabrielle—you will pardon me if I call you Gabrielle, because it is as Gabrielle that I have always thought of you. I beg of you to listen to me, and not to prevaricate, I am your friend—believe it. I come here for you to tell me the truth, so that I may advise you, and help you, before Inspector Gallois arrives."

She was trying desperately to compose herself. Her fingers were tightly interlocked as if they should not betray the desperate nervousness in her heart.

"But still I don't understand. Why should Inspector Gallois come here?" She smiled, "Is it because of the lies which my brother Jules felt himself forced to tell?"

"Yes," he said. "Because of the lies which Jules told, and which Robert told. Even the lies which you yourself told."

Now he was more than ever sure. One word in error and she would have been indignant. All she could pretend was a hurt.

"But, monsieur, what have I done that you should insult me like this?"

He was making a gesture of helplessness and getting to his feet.

"I beg of you not to prevaricate, but you refuse to listen. Do you believe me to be your friend?"

Then there was something lovely about her smile.

"M. Travers, I know you are my friend. What I do not know is this mystery which you continue not to explain."

Travers sat down again. His French, he said, might not be wholly adequate, but it would serve. There were to be moments when he would have to eke it out with English, or a gesture would stand for a phrase, but there was to be scarcely a moment when she did not appear to understand.

"The mystery," he began, "is the murder of a certain Letoque, in the inquiry into which Inspector Gallois and I have, as you know, been concerned. But this Letoque should be given a name which is far better known, His real name—and yet not his real name perhaps, but the name under which he is best known—is Bariche! You know that name?"

She frowned in thought, but her hands, as he saw, were trembling all the same.

"Bariche," she said slowly. "Bariche. There was something in the papers. Yes. He was a Landru, who preyed on women. And wasn't there something else? Didn't he die?"

Travers let out a breath, then was slowly getting to his feet again.

"Perhaps after all we had better await the arrival of Inspector Gallois. And now there is very little time. Already you've wasted ten minutes. You prefer that I should *not* help you. You pretend to know nothing, and all the while Gallois is getting nearer. He won't invite you to say this and that."

"And what *will* he do?" she asked gently. With another helpless shake of the head Travers sat down once more.

"I don't know what he'll do. . . . By this time he's probably had Jules arrested. When he arrives here he may await Robert and then arrest him too, with yourself."

"Arrest! But what for?"

"For the murder of Bariche." He smiled ironically. "You see that once more I invite your confidences, by not referring to him as Letoque."

"But this is absurd! When was this Letoque killed?"

"On the afternoon of Wednesday the ninth of April."

"But we were here, all three of us—even if we should have had any reason for killing this Letoque. We could all swear we were here." Then her eyes were opening wide. "Why, even M. Rabaud knows we were here."

Travers took out his cigarette-case, slowly lighted a cigarette, crossed his long legs and leaned back in the chair. As if she were not there, he was settling himself to wait. A minute passed, and it was she who spoke first.

"M. Travers, I assure you with all my heart that I know you are my friend." A moment's hesitation.

"But it is Robert for whom I am afraid, not for myself. Will you tell me, before he arrives, why it is that you imagine all these things?"

"Very well," he said. "I will begin at what I think is the very beginning. But I warn you that if you lie to me again in defence of any one, I shall stop at once, and it will be to Inspector Gallois that you make your protests. If you wish to question me—do so, remembering always that with every minute we waste, Gallois is on the way here in the car he has hired at Furolles."

He stubbed out the cigarette and drew the chair round till be was almost touching her.

"We begin at your sister—your young sister—Denise, wasn't her name?—who was a widow and who married Bariche, and was about to go abroad. Perhaps you yourself met this sister in Paris, or by some other way you learned that everything was not what it seemed. Robert was here in Lizou already, though you did not join him till a few months ago, and it was to your brother Gaston that you confided your fears. It was he who confronted Bariche at Auteuil. It was he who was shot with your sister, and it was his dead body that was taken for that of Bariche."

Once she had shaken her head quickly, but now, when he paused, she said no word, and her eyes were heavily across the room.

"There was at once a family meeting. For the sake of your mother—then dying, perhaps—nothing was said to the police, and, like others, you preferred to suffer in your hearts rather than disgrace an honourable name. To your friends your sister had married and gone abroad, and Gaston had gone abroad too. Then your mother died and you came here to keep house for Robert. But there was another brother—Jules."

Now it was he who was shaking his head.

"Inspector Gallois will have time to prove everything, but all I can do is to guess, and what I guess is that it was at a famous circus somewhere that your sister first met Bariche. I admit that the papers announced that Bariche had always had a passion for circuses, and it may have been for that reason that Jules decided to accept the offer to become a trapezist. What I am sure of is that all of you must have met this Bariche in Paris—shall we say?—and that then he disappeared with your sister until one of you by chance ran across either him or her. What I insist on is that Jules and Robert must have known Bariche by sight, and all of you—who knew it was Gaston, not Bariche, who had died—

hoped that at some time or other Bariche would visit the Grand Cirque Pertini, and that Jules would recognize him.

"Now I go back to Sunday, the sixth of April. The circus was at Furolles, and you and Robert decided to meet Jules there, rather than, at Carliens where you might be seen by some of your friends from Lizou, I was at the circus that afternoon, and this is what happened. Jules recognized Bariche, who also had gone to the circus, but he recognised him only just before his own act was about to begin. Every one was kept waiting while he found Robert, and pointed out the man who was almost certainly Bariche. Robert followed him, and Jules came to Lizou the next day to hear what happened, though previously, I imagine, he had heard over the 'phone. What he really came for on the Monday was to decide what was to be done about Bariche."

He paused with a smile of grave inquiry.

"So far, am I reasonably right?"

"Please, m'sieu, please! At any moment my brother may come."

"I'm sorry," said Travers. "I did not want to waste time. I'll go straight on from the council of war—shall I call it—which, was held here that Monday afternoon. Undoubtedly it was decided that Bariche deserved fifty deaths, and Robert claimed the right to kill him. Jules decided to keep a watch on him, and to do so he had to sacrifice that pet of his—Auguste, the little white rat—"

"No, no! You are unjust."

She had spoken so vehemently that Travers was Startled.

"But it was given out that Auguste was dead?"

"Perhaps," she said, "but it was unjust to think that Jules killed him." The tired face lighted for a moment. "Jules only pretended he was dead, but he smuggled him here to me. He is in my room, upstairs."

Travers smiled. Neither then not afterwards did it strike him as incongruous that in matters so vital they should pause to discuss the fate of the little tame rat.

"I'm sorry," he said, "I ought to have known that your brother could never have done a thing like that. Even I was upset when I heard that Auguste was dead. But to go on talking about the circus. Jules didn't have to worry about being recognized by Bariche. In the circus Jules was masked, and Bariche would never have suspected that one of your family was a circus artist.

"On the Tuesday morning Jules came here again, and heard about Charles, and saw him. He also reported that he had discovered that Bariche was already having designs on yet another woman, and it was decided to take action at the earliest possible moment. But everything was complicated by Robert's malaria, though doubtless Robert was able to talk things over with both of you. Then who hit on the great scheme I don't know. The scheme however was undoubtedly this.

"Charles was lying up there unconscious that morning, and it was decided to prolong that unconsciousness. Favre was, however, called in for safety and to bolster up the alibi still further. You led Gallois and myself to believe that Favre had come in the afternoon of Tuesday, though I admit you didn't necessarily tell a lie. The word afternoon means many things, according to the time of year. If it is daylight, then it may mean early evening, and that's when Favre did actually come—on the early evening of the Tuesday. *At three o'clock on the afternoon of that Tuesday,* Charles was allowed to recover consciousness, though he was led to believe it was three o'clock *on the Wednesday.* For the Wednesday then, from three o'clock till well after any time which would make any of you concerned in the death of Bariche, all three of you had a perfect alibi."

"But, M. Travers, this is nonsense! it *was* Wednesday. Charles knew it was Wednesday. He saw the Wednesday's newspaper, and that would have been impossible on the Tuesday"

The eyes of Travers opened wide. Now he knew why Gallois had gone into Charles's room at midnight and asked about the newspaper.

"But why prevaricate? Charles, it is true, was shown a newspaper, but he did not examine that newspaper, he was merely shown it—like this. But I say, and you know, that the things that were then supposed to happen on the Wednesday, really happened on the Tuesday—except one, Favre did come here when Charles was sent to sleep again. He's an old man and careless perhaps, and he accepted all that he was told. He saw Charles lying under the influence of a sedative or drug, and he made no examination. Charles, as far as he was concerned, had not recovered consciousness, but to him it appeared that he was likely at any time to do so, and he was in no danger.

"Charles then was kept sleeping till just before I arrived here with your brother on the Wednesday evening, I expect Jules telephoned you from Gevrol that we had just arrived there, and it would be safe to let Charles come round again. Charles woke up, feeling better *after what he thought was a two-hour nap,* but he had been sleeping or unconscious since the previous Tuesday afternoon."

He paused and tried to catch her eye, but always she was looking away across to the window. Her face seemed suddenly older and very tired, and her hands were limp in her lap.

"Will you tell me what happened at the Villa Sablons?" he said.

She shook her head quickly.

"Perhaps it was this, then," he went on. "Charles had told you on the Tuesday that Gallois must be met at Toulon. Someone had to go to Toulon then on the Wednesday, and it could not be Jules. Then Robert, who should have killed Bariche, was too ill with his malaria, and it was you who volunteered to kill Bariche. You insisted that you should be identified with this cause, as much as the others and up to the very hilt. You claimed the right, perhaps, on behalf of your dead sister. Your brothers knew you, and they trusted you. That Wednesday night. Robert was so proud of what you had done, that he boasted of you to me and Gallois, and of your bravery and your courage in a crisis.

"What was arranged then was this, and I frankly confess I don't know if Robert was well enough at the time to be told all of it. You rang Bariche and told him I don't know what—except perhaps that you were an unknown admirer—while Jules gave a free ticket for the circus to the woman in the house. But then Robert was suddenly feeling better, and wished perhaps to kill Bariche after all, while you went to Toulon. But, as was pointed out, Bariche was now expecting a woman. To receive a man might make him slam the door in the caller's face. Therefore it was you who went to the Villa Sablons to avenge your sister and brother. You left the Villa afterwards by the way Jules had mapped out for you, and, while you were there, it was Jules who watched Charles. Before you were back, Robert had left for Toulon in a hired car. As soon as you reached here from Carliens, you punctured your own car as arranged."

He touched her gently, and his look had an infinite pity.

"All this is true? . . . For this moment, between you and me?"

"Perhaps," she said. She spoke so softly that he scarcely heard, and her smile was strangely calm. "And even if it were so, I still do not understand how you came to know."

"There were things you forgot," he said, and almost with regret. "Charles insisted to myself and Gallois that when he first awoke it was unnaturally calm. That was what struck him—the peace of the little room up there. There was not even a mosquito that buzzed or a fly that stirred, it was so peaceful. But when he awoke again after what he thought was only a nap, it was not quiet. The air was full of the noise of animals going home from the fair. But, as I came to realize, if he had woke that Wednesday afternoon, he would still have heard the sound of people and animals. One cannot hold a great fair within four hundred metres of a house without hearing the noise of people and animals. Also he did hear the clock in the church tower, and that's more than four hundred metres away.

"Later there was something else, which perhaps does not matter. While he was unconscious, Charles dreamt that he was in the sea and always trying to reach the surface, and at last something seemed to break on his brain and there he was on the surface—in the bed. To me that doesn't seem like an unconsciousness that was natural. It was as if he was drugged again and again—harmlessly, perhaps—just when he was on the point of waking up."

She had not heard the last words, for she had sprung to her feet and was flying to the porch. Robert Debran was about to draw his car in at the side lane, and she was calling.

"Robert, quick! Get me something from the village."

He saw the doctor shrug his shoulders and back the car out again. What it was that she wanted he could not hear, but in a minute she was in the room.

"Quick, m'sieu, I beg of you. In five minutes he will be back."

"There's nothing else to say," he told her. "Only this perhaps. You were alarmed that Wednesday night when you heard who Gallois was, but Robert reassured you. Nevertheless in the morning you set our breakfast table under this very window out there, while you were in this room listening, and dreading that something might be said by either of us to reveal that we had suspicions. Also you didn't want us to go to Carliens where we should hear about the murder. You even kept the newspaper from us that morning. You wanted us to stay here, and the following morning when Charles went away with us, you wanted all of us to go right away to Mariette. Anywhere rather than Carliens."

As she sank down in the chair, he wondered for a moment if she were going to faint. But she was still smiling wanly, and shaking her head.

"But if all this is true, why should you come here? Why did you not leave us to this M. Gallois?"

He turned away.

"I don't know. It's the hardest thing to explain to you. Perhaps I didn't want you to lie to Gallois. I didn't want the three of you to commit perjury and swear lies on behalf of each other. It was you above all I did not want to be guilty of that."

Her hand was timidly on his arm.

"But if I killed Bariche, wouldn't it be a small thing to lie—after that?"

"Perhaps," he said. "Perhaps also I'm a fool. There are things that shame one and bring disgrace, and I might be the kind of fool who agreed with the killing of Bariche."

Her eyes suddenly narrowed and her whole body was taut.

"If it were to be done again to-morrow, I would do it. The law had done nothing, and he was not fit to live."

There was silence for a long minute. Travers was thinking of that Wednesday evening, and all the anxieties that Robert must have been undergoing as he went to Toulon, and waited there, and came back. He could hear his voice that night when Gabrielle came to the porch. "Everything goes well?" "Yes," she had told him serenely. "Everything goes well—very well."

A murderess, he was thinking, and the assassin of Bariche. And yet he did not know.

To him she would always be something other than that. And then a sound was heard. His startled eyes met the calm eyes of Gabrielle.

"It is M. Gallois," she said gently.

"Remain here," he told her quickly. "Let me see him first. Believe me when I say I will do all I can."

It was a hired car, or a police car from Furolles, for two men sat in the back, and to them Gallois was giving instructions. Travers stood impassively by, and it was not till one of the men made a move that be spoke.

"One minute!"

Gallois turned startledly, then slowly got out of the car.

"Remain here," he told the men, and as Travers moved off across the grass he was following him. On went Travers to the far side of the house till they were out of earshot.

"You forgive me?" Travers said.

But it was the face of Gallois that showed humiliation.

"I should have known," he said. "We are affinities, you and I, and what one thinks the other thinks also. And you came here to meet me?"

"Yes," said Travers. "And to hear the truth for myself."

Gallois nodded, and his lean face took on a seriousness.

"Jules is arriving from Nice. The others are here?"

"Robert is coming at any moment," Travers said. "But Gabrielle, you won't question her if she confesses? I've tortured her too much myself already."

Gallois nodded again.

"My friend, it shall be as you ask. And you, you prefer to wait here?"

"Yes," said Travers. "But one moment. What will they do to her? Surely they can't send her to the guillotine?"

The smile of Gallois had in it a knowledge of the sorrows of all mankind.

"Two years, perhaps. One year—who knows? There will be sympathies. Perhaps there will not even be one year. Who can tell?"

A slow shake of the head and he was making for the door. Travers stood for a moment, glasses in his motionless hands. As he blinked in the glare of that hot noonday sun, he vaguely discerned at the already open door a something that would be Gabrielle. But he heard the voices, and it was hers that was the more calm.

"It is you then, M. Gallois."

"Yes," said Gallois gravely. "It is I."

And that was all. When Travers hooked the glasses on again the two were already in the house. What he was feeling he hardly knew, but there was a sense of intrusion on the tragedies of others, and something like a vague shame, and as the sound of the doctor's car was heard, there was something that was also like fear, and on a sudden impulse he was turning away, and his hands once more went fumblingly to his glasses.

THE END

www.ingramcontent.com/pod-product-compliance
Lightning Source LLC
Chambersburg PA
CBHW071820190726
48292CB00005B/1528